COTTON CANDY

COTTON CANDY

Jean Morley

*For Eileen
Happy reading
Jean Morley*

iUniverse, Inc.
New York Lincoln Shanghai

Cotton Candy

Copyright © 2005 by Jean Morley

All rights reserved. No part of this book may be used or reproduced by any means, graphic, electronic, or mechanical, including photocopying, recording, taping or by any information storage retrieval system without the written permission of the publisher except in the case of brief quotations embodied in critical articles and reviews.

iUniverse books may be ordered through booksellers or by contacting:

iUniverse
2021 Pine Lake Road, Suite 100
Lincoln, NE 68512
www.iuniverse.com
1-800-Authors (1-800-288-4677)

ISBN-13: 978-0-595-35107-7 (pbk)
ISBN-13: 978-0-595-79809-4 (ebk)
ISBN-10: 0-595-35107-7 (pbk)
ISBN-10: 0-595-79809-8 (ebk)

Printed in the United States of America

Chapter 1

▼

It was hot, very hot. It was so hot that all was quiet and nothing stirred as no one or no thing could be bothered to move or make a sound. Those who lived in the large Georgian plantation house called Farrell Hall were no exception, as it could be seen that Thomas Farrell's four daughters were in their own room, which was the coolest room in the house. This was because the house was built in the best possible position facing the Ashley River, from whence any breezes there were wafted over the great expanse of lawn and gardens before reaching the rooms inside the house itself.

The girls' room, decorated in pale pinks and white, had evidently progressed from being a playroom for very young children to one for young ladies. It was furnished simply with footstools, sofas and comfortable chairs in a jumble of colours. The old oak table which was in the centre of the room was at this moment covered with a cloth on which stood sewing boxes, books, magazines, a basket of fruit and a jug of fruit juice.

As it was so hot the girls were dressed in loose cotton robes of white and three of them were sitting quietly reading and moving as little as possible. Emma at seventeen was a pretty, delicately featured girl with a gentle manner. Her large brown eyes looked calmly on anyone who was kind to her and she had been a very popular partner at the social dances held in Charleston the previous winter. She favoured her mother, now sadly departed, after whom she was named. At the moment she was looking at the latest fashion magazine.

Opposite her sat Charlotte, named after her paternal grandmother, but not at all like her, either in looks or disposition. At fifteen she was a plump young lady with a round face and a ready smile that usually brought answering ones from people she met. She was also down to earth in her manner, but in spite of this she was popular and was to become even more so as she became older. At the moment she was immersed in reading a novel, which, if her papa had been present, he would have immediately taken away from her, deeming it not fit for her to read. As far as her older sisters were concerned, though, it kept her quiet and happy so they left her alone.

The youngest of the group was Caroline. She was named after South Carolina, the state in which they lived, but her name was usually shortened to Carrie. She was lying on her stomach on one of the sofas and, in this unladylike position with her legs waving about gently in the air, making an effort to keep cool. She was fourteen and hardly ever still. A pretty, slim girl with dark eyes, she was finding life difficult without her mama. She was often in trouble, like falling from a tree she had climbed or not helping her sisters when requested and hiding herself. She liked to make life uncomfortable for them, if she could. Her papa, though, was kindness itself, even spoiling her in his attempt to make up to her for the loss of her mama. Her sisters hoped she would soon pass out of this difficult stage and bore with her as best they could. Carrie was now trying to read an improving book without much success.

The eldest of them all was Christie. She was named, as was the custom for the eldest girl, with her maternal grandmother's maiden name. She was eighteen, dark haired and the only one in the family with dark blue eyes. These were set in a serious face, although the times when she did smile or laugh transformed her completely into an attractive young lady. She tried to be a mother to the younger ones with Emma's help, after mama, a kind and frail lady, had died two years previously during the 'dying months'. These were the summer months when fevers and disease abounded. So it was up to Christie, now, to sort out any problems that occurred and run the house for them all. Her father, of course, was still able to keep an eye on things as well, although he was mainly interested in the running of his cotton plantation. At this moment Christie just sat with a frown on her face as if she were trying to sort out a problem.

Her thoughts, though, were interrupted by Carrie who broke the silence by throwing down her book and declaring: 'I don't feel like reading stuffy old books. It's too hot.' She turned over and stretched luxuriously. 'Can't we have the boys in to fan us?'

'The boys' she referred to were the two youngest black servants who waved the large fans to and fro in an effort to keep the family comfortable in the hot weather, when requested. Christie came out of her reverie.

'No,' she said firmly. 'Papa is resting and needs them, probably. Besides, if he doesn't, they need time to rest too. They feel the heat as much as we do, you know, and they don't have a cool room like this to be in.'

'But they are servants,' argued Carrie.

'It's about time you realised, Miss, that if you treat servants properly, the better they serve you,' answered Christie sharply. 'You can bathe in the river later when it's cooler, if you like.'

Carrie sniffed and ignored her, her face taking on a mulish expression.

'I don't know whether I want to,' she muttered.

It was quiet for some time after that apart from Carrie playing with her hair ribbon, uttering sighs and wriggling about on the sofa. Even Emma began to feel irritated and reprimanded her younger sister by saying mildly, 'Carrie, dear, do behave like a young lady should. If you want something to do, why don't you sit quietly and mend the hem of your gown?'

'Oh, Em, you know my stitching is terrible,' she whined. 'Do it for me please, your stitches are so much neater.'

'You'll never make a good wife,' Emma remarked.

Her remark reminded Carrie of something. With a glint in her eye she said, 'Christie?'

'Mmm?'

'When are you going to marry Joel?'

Christie looked up, surprised. 'I—I don't know. Why?'

'Do you mean he hasn't asked you yet or you really don't know? I thought it was all arranged.'

'Well,' said Christie, 'it's arranged, I think, between Papa and Mr Winthrop, Joel's Papa, but nothing has been said between Joel and myself.'

'Well,' said Carrie innocently, 'can't you ask Joel? I think you should hurry him up. He's so handsome. Other girls think so too. You might lose him, you know, if you don't get on with it.'

'Thank you, for your concern, Carrie. I'll let you know what happens.' Christie answered in such a way that forbade her sister to say any more.

Emma smiled. 'Oh Carrie,' she said.

Charlotte by this time had closed her book. She had finished it and was looking all starry eyed. 'What's this about getting married? That's what I've just been reading about.' She pressed her hands together. 'Ooh, it's so romantic, isn't it?'

'Christie doesn't think so,' grinned Carrie. 'She hasn't made her mind up about Joel yet.'

'Not made her mind up? Why? Has he asked her then?'

'Don't let us go into all that again,' said Christie. 'For goodness' sake find something useful to do instead of talking nonsense, you two.'

Carrie and Charlotte made a face at each other and nodded knowingly, but before any further comments could be made a tap sounded on the door.

'Come in,' chorused the girls.

A young black servant put her head round the door. 'Please, Miss Christie, Massa says he wants you to be ready in half an hour.'

'Thank you,' said Christie as the door closed. She stretched, sighed and rose out of her chair. 'Anyone want to accompany Papa and me?' she asked.

'Too hot,' came the answer from Emma and Carrie, but Charlotte looked up. 'I wouldn't mind,' she said. 'I'd like to see the children.'

'Good. Come along then, we'd better change into something neat and tidy and then visit Zilpah.'

It was twenty minutes later that the two girls, looking refreshed, tripped down the stairs to the servants' quarters to find Zilpah, a plump black lady who liked to wear a brightly coloured scarf tied around her head.

'Zilpah!' called Christie.

'I'm here, Miss Christie. You want fruit for de children?'

'Yes, please. Is the basket ready?'

'It sure is, Miss Christie. Is Jacob to get de carriage out? Mis' Farrell didn't say.'

'What do you think, Charlotte? Can we manage the basket between us?'

'I'd rather walk,' said Charlotte. 'It's a little cooler now and I've sat still too long this afternoon.'

'Thank you Zilpah, we'll manage, then. We'll meet Papa by the front door.' So they went from the yard where the water pump stood and where the carriages and horse were stabled, to meet their father.

They only had a few minutes to wait before Thomas Farrell joined them. He was a kindly looking man and in his early fifties. Although of only medium height he looked taller as he held himself well. He was a good and shrewd businessman and employed a secretary and an accountant to help him run the plantation. It had been a bitter blow to him when his wife had died but his daughters, especially Christie, had been a great comfort to him. In earlier days he had hoped for a son to help and carry on the cotton business but evidently it had not been God's wish. Christie, however, was very helpful and hardworking, and hopefully some time soon, she would marry Joel.

The Winthrop plantation ran alongside the Farrells' and Thomas hoped that in the future the two would amalgamate and bring in even more wealth. He felt he must provide for all his daughters' futures and dowries and also his possible grandchildren.

Now he smiled as he saw Christie and Charlotte waiting for him. 'How nice to have two charming young ladies to accompany me,' he smiled.

So side-by-side and carrying the basket of fruit between them, they set off across the wide expanse of lawn and further, with Charlotte giggling at the compliment.

Chapter 2

The ten brick built cabins where the slaves lived stood in a clearing not far from the cotton fields where they worked. They consisted of one room only and each one housed a family but often more lived there. Those that were young enough, men and women, worked in the cotton fields. The older people mended fences, spun cotton and looked after the children until they were ten years old when they too would work in the fields. Depending on the season the cotton had to be planted, weeded, hoed, manured, picked and then the earth had to be cleared ready to start all over again. Eventually, the cotton was sent on its way to be bought in other parts of the country or shipped overseas.

Families were often broken up and sold on for one reason or another, such as a payment of debt or because they would fetch a good price at market. Thomas Farrell had never done this, however. He bought well in the first place, treated them reasonably well and without cruelty, which resulted in good workers and therefore good profits.

Thomas Farrell's slaves, or workers, as he preferred to call them, used a task system. Not all plantation owners implemented this method but he found it worked well as there was no need for an overseer and so there was far less supervision. Some plantations had overseers who were quite happy to use whips, sometimes mercilessly, when they felt like it or when they believed a particular slave was lazy or had misbehaved in some way. But that was not Thomas's way. He was not a violent man and he preferred to treat his family, servants and workers fairly. Consequently they were happier and therefore worked better.

One of the first workers he bought was a giant of a fellow whom he had named Joseph. He found he worked well. Now, some twenty years later he happily left him in charge as he had proved capable and popular with his own people. Thomas visited him every day to view the progress and tell him what he expected to be done the following day. If the work was finished in good time the rest of the day was for the workers to do with as they wished. They had been given some land and were allowed to cultivate their own plots and either use the produce themselves or sell it at market on a Sunday for which they had to obtain a pass from Thomas.

The women would also go to market on a Sunday with the baskets that they had made. They picked the sweet grass that grew in the water and treated it so that it could be woven. From start to finish the process of making a basket took about fifteen hours but the results were attractive and varied and also serviceable. Those that they did not keep for themselves were sold.

Just now they were all back from the fields and one of the young boys, who had been told to keep watch, ran to Joseph to tell him that he could see 'Massa' and ladies approaching. Joseph, showing his white teeth in a welcoming grin went forward to meet them, while the older children stood in groups, watching and waiting. The little ones, wanting to join in but too shy to do so, clung to their mothers, their thumbs in their mouths.

Thomas waved a hand to everyone and then went with Joseph to view the work that had been accomplished that day and to discuss how much could be achieved on the next. Meanwhile, Christie and Charlotte moved forward and began to distribute the fruit. After a while, Christie left her sister to carry on and quietly told her not to forget to make a game of the cookies that she expected Zilpah had hidden underneath. Christie had begun this to make the children laugh by pretending to be surprised when she found the cookies. She would say they were all for her and they must not have them. Then she pretended to think and hand one to a child, then she would decide another could have one and so on until all were distributed. The children would laugh, knowing this is what she would do. They liked the ritual.

While Charlotte was busy with the children Christie visited their parents and the older men and women to see if there were any problems. Thomas insisted their welfare was important if they were to work well. So Christie endeavoured to sort out any problems that Joseph was unable to, as well as any medical ones. A few years previous there had been a case when one woman was having difficulty in childbirth. Joseph had walked over to the 'big house', something that was only done in an emergency, to see if Thomas was able to help. Thomas sent for his doctor who sorted out the problem, which resulted in a healthy boy and a relieved and grateful mother.

Christie tried to have a few words with everyone if she could so no one was ignored. However, on this day everything seemed well enough and she was just turning away to find her sister when a voice called softly, 'Miss?' Christie looked round to find a young girl standing apart from the others. She was a pretty girl, a well developed fourteen year old, who looked shyly at her. Christie smiled at her reassuringly.

'Did you want to talk to me?' she asked. The girl nodded but did not move. 'Come and sit down,' Christie said, leading the way to a spot beneath one of the old oak trees that overshadowed the buildings and helped to keep them cool. She sat on the ground and patted the place next to her. The girl sat down, her fingers playing with her cotton skirt.

'Well?' asked Christie.

The girl looked up. 'Do white men come?' she whispered, her eyes dark and frightened.

Christie was puzzled. 'There are no white men here except Mr Farrell and he speaks only to Joseph. Are you worried about other white men?'

The girl nodded.

'Have you seen any others here?' Christie asked, wondering if her father had taken anyone to see the cotton fields without mentioning the fact to the family.

But the girl shook her head. 'I hear,' she said.

'What did you hear?'

The girl shrugged.

'It frightens you?' The girl nodded.

Christie frowned. 'I see. I'll find out. As far as I know, no white man will bother you. If you are worried, tell Joseph. You understand?'

The girl nodded with a little smile.

Meanwhile, Charlotte had enjoyed her time with the children and left them with grins on their faces. She loved the little plump ones with their mass of curly hair and the slim legged older ones with their dazzling white smiles. She found them fascinating. She must come and see them more often. It was fun.

As Thomas and his daughters made their way back to the Hall, Charlotte chattered to her father telling him about the children. Thomas listened, pleased she had enjoyed herself and hoped she would do it again to relieve Christie of some of the responsibility. He noticed his older daughter was quiet and asked the reason. She told him about the young girl.

'There's no white men around as far as I know,' said her father. 'And if there are I want to know why and who they are. But perhaps she misinterpreted something she heard the others say?'

Christie thought this possible so said no more.

They returned to the house to find Emma and Carrie looking neat and clean, having changed into clean dresses, and awaiting the others. Carrie had been experimenting with her long tresses yet again and this time, with the help of pins and combs, had her hair piled up on her head. It all looked rather top heavy over her young face, and ready to fall down at any minute. Her father noticed but he kept a straight face, only looking at Christie and winking. No one made any comment, they just accepted Carrie's childish efforts at attention seeking and left her alone.

Christie and Charlotte hurried to change yet again as the bell would soon sound heralding dinnertime. Eventually the four girls assembled in the dining room, standing behind their respective chairs to await their father. All wore silk dresses, not cut too low, as Papa objected but a light fichu was allowed if necessary. Emma's dress was of pale blue with a darker blue quilted underskirt decorated with tiny white flowers. Carrie's dress was in white as befitted a young girl and Charlotte favoured a deep rose pink with a cream underskirt. Christie wore her favourite port wine coloured dress, in which she looked quite dramatic had she realised the fact, with her serious face and jet black hair. All the girls wore stomachers and their hair, which was long, was dressed simply either in ringlets or, as in Christie's case, just tied back. Carrie, of course, was the exception but her Papa would let her get away with it as long as it pleased her. Thomas, dressed as usual in black knee breeches and coat, always insisted on keeping high standards; low ones encouraged servants to slovenly habits.

Usually conversation over dinner consisted of the day's happenings and arrangements made for the next day if necessary. It was a lengthy business as Thomas liked it to be a relaxed time and a special family time. Afterwards, prayers were held, to which servants were expected to attend. This only lasted ten minutes at the most, with Thomas giving thanks for the day, a prayer for all the people he was responsible for and a special one for his dear departed wife. Then while the servants cleared away, Thomas and the girls would retire to the withdrawing room to talk, read or play such board games as chess or fox and geese before bedtime.

However, on this particular day Thomas asked Christie to accompany him to his study. He wished to talk to her privately.

'Now, my dear,' he said when they were both comfortably sitting down, 'you are eighteen. I feel it is time you were married, you know.'

'Do you, Papa?' she said with a laugh. 'Do you want to be rid of me so soon?'

Thomas smiled. 'I shall miss you, of course, and certainly the help that you give me. Hopefully the others, Charlotte and Carrie could take your place in some respects. Emma, I fear, is delicate, as her Mama was, but she would be good around the house like she is already. However, I'm hoping you won't be far away from us.' He looked directly at his daughter.

'Not far away?' asked Christie.

'I'm thinking of Joel, Christie.'

Christie looked down at her hands. 'Ah,' was all she said.

'You know the Winthrops expect it. Wilbur and I talked of the joining of the two properties eventually when he and I are old and no longer able to control them. It would leave Joel and you in charge. You know how to deal with the workers and I'm sure Joel does too. You've both been brought up to know how to go on so I can't see any problem.'

Christie did not answer straightaway but sat looking at her hands.

'Papa, have you seen Mr Winthrop or Joel lately? Have they mentioned this?'

'As a matter of fact, no. Why?'

'Well, I haven't seen Joel at all apart from a dance in the wintertime, so I cannot think he is that keen to be with me. Also, I haven't visited the Winthrops' house since we were all children. I know we live near but that doesn't mean we know them well.'

'Don't you like Joel?'

'I don't know him, Papa. I know we all played together as children but he and his brothers were all older than we were so we didn't have that much to do with them. I think we really went with Mama when she visited Mrs Winthrop. When I did meet Joel last he was friendly and I agree in a way he's attractive, but all the other girls seemed to think so too and were always round him. Has he been away, do you think?'

'He could have been. I don't know. Would you be agreeable to meeting him here one evening if I arranged it?'

'Yes, of course, Papa.'

'Then that is what we'll do. We'll invite them to dine with us.'

They returned to join the others but Thomas only bade them all 'good night' and retired either to write a letter to Wilbur or to go to bed for an early night's sleep. The intense heat during the day took its toll now he was no longer young but he felt pleased that he could eventually pass the reins over to two young people who would carry on the business and who knew what they were doing. If anything happened that he wasn't able to cope with any more, then the family would be secure and in good hands. He frowned. It was true what Christie had said.

Although they lived next door to each other, meaning a few miles apart, as the plantations covered a vast area, neither the Farrells nor the Winthrops had been in favour of visiting or encroaching on each other's land. It was different when the children were small. His wife had visited Wilbur's and taken the girls with her. The Winthrops had had three boys who were more mature. He seemed to remember the older ones left some time ago, leaving the youngest, Joel, at home. Also, that they had renounced their inheritance and moved away to marry and live abroad. Joel must be about twenty-four now, just the right age for Christie. He had been surprised that she had said that she hardly knew him, though, but then, since his wife Emma had died, Christie had had no one to take her visiting. He wondered why Joel showed no interest in his daughter. To her father's eyes she was attractive, even beautiful—and hard working. Still, that all might be amended when they met at the dinner he planned to give.

Christie, meanwhile, had sat down with the others once more with a frown on her face and her thoughts elsewhere. After some minutes, the girls, who had stopped whatever they were doing to gaze hopefully at her and to share any news she had to impart, looked at one another when that news was not forthcoming. It was Carrie, impatient as ever, who gave a loud cough, hoping that it would break into Christie's thoughts. It did. She looked up, a faraway expression on her face.

'Well?' asked Carrie and Charlotte.

'Oh—er, Papa is arranging a dinner here for Mr and Mrs Winthrop and Joel.' She said it so seriously with no smile or twinkle in her dark eyes.

'You don't sound very pleased about it, dear,' said Emma softly. 'Why are they invited?'

'For—for me to meet Joel. Papa seemed to think I know him. Like you, I've seen him and he was there when we used to visit with Mama. But I don't *know* him.'

'I've seen him,' piped up Carrie. 'I think he's ever so handsome.'

'But looks don't make a good husband, dear,' said Emma.

'The trouble is,' went on Christie, 'Papa wants the two plantations to amalgamate so it will be security for us all. If I don't marry Joel, I shall be responsible for you all and...'

Charlotte interrupted. 'Well, we could manage if we all helped. We still have Mr Pope who does the paperwork for Papa and Mr Page who writes the letters and things. Joseph and the other workers are no trouble if we treat them well!'

Christie smiled. 'You make it sound so simple, Charlotte. But thank you because what you are really saying is that if I don't like Joel, I won't have to marry him?'

Charlotte nodded. 'I suppose so. It can't be very comfortable to be married to someone you don't like.'

'Well, we'll see,' said Christie, smiling at last. 'You never know, he might take a fancy to one of you instead of me. Have you thought of that?'

The mood lightened and they all giggled; a few more preposterous comments were made about who Joel would be likely to choose and why.

Then Christie said it was her bedtime, kissed her sisters goodnight and made her way up the beautiful floating staircase, while the girls below enjoyed a cosy tête-à-tête on the topic of husbands.

Chapter 3

Christie awoke the next morning feeling decidedly jaded. Why was it, she wondered? She sat up and rubbed her eyes, pushing her long hair away. Also her head ached. Then she remembered sleep had eluded her and she had spent half the night tossing and turning. It wasn't the heat—she was used to that—it was the conversation with her father about her possible forthcoming marriage that had disturbed her. She knew at the back of her mind that being wedded to Joel had always been a possibility and it had never worried her, as the event seemed a long way off. Now it was imminent, it was a different matter entirely. Did she want to marry Joel if she had a choice? She hardly knew him. That could be remedied, of course, but did she want to marry anyone at all just yet? She didn't think she did. She couldn't disappoint her father though, and the welfare of her sisters all hung on her acceptance, whatever Charlotte said. Dear Charlotte!

There was a knock on the door and the maid brought in her hot chocolate and another appeared with water for washing in a tall brass jug. After they left, Christie took a few sips only from her cup and decided to get up. It was no good going over and over the things in her mind any more. 'Forget it all for now,' she told herself. 'Think about it again after breakfast when your head is clear and you feel better.'

The girls usually had their first meal of the day in the breakfast parlour together, leaving Thomas to have his in his room or where and when he chose. This morning, as usual, Charlotte and Carrie ate as though they hadn't seen food for a week. In between mouthfuls they managed to chat to each other, giggling at some private joke and making plans for the day. Emma, preferring a slower start to her day, sat in a dream world of her own, nibbling toast and stirring her coffee.

So it was a relief to Christie that they did not notice her heavy eyes and pale face. Also that she wasn't as bright as usual. However, she managed a reasonable breakfast which pleased her, as she told herself there was no need to skimp on food just because she was worried. So, feeling much better, as she had sensibly predicted for herself, Christie rose from the table with one clear idea in her mind, which was to visit Grandmama Farrell.

'I'm going into Charleston,' she announced. 'Does anyone want to shop or…'

Carrie interrupted, saying impetuously, 'Charlotte, shall we go and visit Mary and Jem? We haven't seen them for ages.'

Charlotte nodded. 'Ooh, yes. That would be very pleasant.'

Emma said in a vague way that she would stay home as she had things to do. So Christie went downstairs to find Zilpah.

'Morning, Miss Christie,' said Zilpah with a wide grin when she saw her. Then she looked harder. 'You look nohow,' she said.

'I didn't sleep very well.'

'Uh-huh! Problems?'

'Something like that. I'm going to see Grandmama.'

'Good,' said Zilpah.

'Oh, Zilpah, I must warn you. My father will be hosting a dinner for Mr and Mrs Winthrop and their son soon. The date has yet to be decided but I thought you should be warned.'

Zilpah nodded. She looked at Christie. 'Is dat what's troubling you? I can make good dinner.'

'Oh Zilpah I know you can. No, no, it's not that.'

'Well, if your Gran'ma can't help, you come and tell old Zilpah. I known you a long time.'

'Oh, Zilpah, you've always been here. And you're not so old either,' Christie said with a smile.

'Mm,' said Zilpah, hunching a plump shoulder. 'Old enough to be your mama.'

In that she was right for she was one of the first slaves Thomas Farrell had bought. She had been for sale with the others. She was about fifteen years old then and heavily pregnant. She had evidently married in Africa but her husband was not with her any more. Either he had escaped the 'white men' or been taken into slavery elsewhere. They had all come from the Gold Coast in Africa. To the traders they were known as 'black gold.'

Zilpah had stood there with the others until she was the last to be taken. She was a thin and pregnant, sickly girl, a butt for jokes from the white men buying.

But Thomas had bought her as she looked so terrified and he had felt sorry for her. She had come to the Hall along with Joseph and the others. Thomas's wife said she was to be placed up at the house and not work in the fields. She could eventually work in the kitchen. So she was taken care of until Jacob was born. Zilpah then established herself in the household, especially after Mrs Farrell had died. Zilpah would do anything for Thomas and his motherless girls. He had taken pity on her and had been kind to her and helped her. Now she would do the same for him and his family.

Christie said, 'I'm taking Charlotte and Carrie to visit some friends first. Do you need anything from the shops, Zilpah?'

She told Christie what she required and then found Jacob, telling him to be ready with the small open carriage to take the ladies into town.

It was pleasant out, the heat not yet too oppressive. Jacob, now an attractive young man, sat up proudly driving the horse with the young ladies in the carriage dressed in pretty cotton dresses, with bonnets to match and holding their parasols. Twenty minutes later they came to the outskirts of the small town of Charleston where the streets were tree lined and cool. Charlotte and Carrie were delivered to their friend's house but Christie waited until she knew it was convenient for them to stay. Carrie came running back to say they were invited to lunch and would be taken back home later in the day. Christie nodded and told Jacob to carry on to the shops in order to purchase the commodities for Zilpah.

There was a bustle of buyers at the market stalls who preferred shopping in the cooler mornings to the intense heat of the afternoons. These were for sitting with cool drinks and being fanned. But it was a colourful picture with customers in their pretty coloured dresses with some gentlemen accompanying them but mostly with their black servants in attendance.

Christie saw no one she knew. Apart from the few friends she visited occasionally, some of whom were her mother's friends, she found she had no opportunity to meet anyone new. That had to be left for the later, cooler months when she could attend socials and mix with other young people. Of course, with their mother dying, she and her sisters hadn't had great opportunities for mixing as they had been in mourning for a year. This meant no social gatherings, only quiet conversations with friends who called. It had been difficult to adjust to their new life after this.

Christie brought her thoughts back to the present. The shopping done, they drove to Grandmama Farrell's. She lived in a town house that was small, as far as Christie was concerned, but it really was of a comfortable size. The carriage stopped outside where sculpted stone pineapples topped the gateposts either side of the wrought iron gates. New and exotic fruits from unknown continents had been brought to the American colonies, the pineapple being the favourite because of its delicious taste. Therefore it was the most highly favoured among the fruits. It was now a symbol of hospitality and many were seen in all sizes outside houses and often carved on furniture inside.

The door opened in answer to her knock to reveal a servant standing there. He smiled when he saw who it was. As Christie stepped inside the tiled entrance hall, a black woman came bustling through.

'Matty,' called Christie. 'Is Grandmama well? Could I see her, do you think?'

'Yes, Miss Christie. She's had her breakfast and is now sitting in the parlour smoking those dratted cigar things. Makes everywhere smell awful and then she wonders why she coughs. I have no patience with her.'

For all her strictures Christie knew Matty took good care of her mistress and would do anything for her.

'I'll open the window for a while,' said Christie as she prepared to climb the stairs.

'Huh,' sniffed Matty, with a look that implied she didn't hold out much hope, disappearing into the nether regions of the house.

Christie knocked on the door and went in.

'Good morning, Grandmama. I see you're looking well.' She bent over the little scrap of a figure that reclined on the chaise longue and kissed her cheek.

Christie's grandmother was dressed in a gown of lavender silk and her silver hair was tied back with a ribbon to match. Her lined face was powdered and rouged and the hand that held the small cheroot was wrinkled. Her misshapen fingers were adorned with many rings. Blue eyes surveyed Christie.

'Oh, it's you. Are you alone?'

'Yes, Grandmama. Jacob came with me to shop and we also took the children to their friend's house. Now Jacob is seeing to the horse and no doubt enjoying himself in your kitchen.'

'What's wrong, then?'

'Nothing's wrong, Grandmama.'

'I'm not stupid although I look senile. You wouldn't come alone if you weren't in trouble of some kind or another. Have you been misbehaving with some young man and now you're in the family way? Out with it, girl. And stop opening the window. It will be hot in here before you can blink. I'll put this thing out if you can't stand the smell. Sit down.'

Christie sat, saying 'Really Grandmama, you….'

'Mustn't say those kind of things? I call a spade a spade. I can't do with missishness or namby pamby people around me. Now,' she fixed Christie once more with her gimlet eyes. 'What's worrying you? You look awful.'

'I don't look as bad as that, do I?'

'Yes.'

'Well, it's—it's because I didn't sleep very well last night, that's all.'

'So, why didn't you sleep last night?'

'I—I'm slightly worried.'

Charlotte Farrell looked at her granddaughter for a second. Then she said with a sigh: 'Christie, don't let me have to 'chip away at the rock to find the diamond'. For goodness' sake, tell me, girl.' She waited expectantly.

Christie, now looking as though she would burst into tears any minute, swallowed hard.

Her Grandmother said kindly: 'Help yourself to a drink, then come and sit next to me.' She moved to a sitting position and patted the seat next to her. So Christie did as she was told and found a small, frail hand gripping hers quite strongly.

'Now, tell me,' her Grandmama said softly.

'Well, Papa thinks it is time I was married,' began Christie.

'How old are you now?'

'I'm eighteen.'

Her Grandmama nodded. 'Quite right. I was married at eighteen. A good age for a girl to marry. Have you met someone then? Do I know the family? Where did you meet him? Go on, tell me.'

'Well, no—no, it's not like that. You see, apart from a few social occasions I've attended or if we all are invited out, I don't meet a lot of people. Since Mama died I'm busy seeing that things run smoothly in the house and then I go to see the workers with Papa and look after their welfare. And Papa discusses things with me about the plantation so that I know all about it. Which means I don't have much time to meet many young men apart from the workers, of course. Then there are the girls to care for, especially Carrie. Emma helps, of course, and Papa is very good with her. Zilpah is a treasure too.'

'Huh! It sounds to me that your Father treats you like the son he never had one minute and a substitute companion the next. I'll speak to him.'

'Oh, Grandmama, no, no, please don't do that. I don't mind doing all those things, I'm not complaining. I quite enjoy what I do, but…'

'But?'

'Well,' smiled Christie wistfully. 'I would like to do some fun things sometimes and travel a little before I marry. You see, Papa would like me to marry Joel Winthrop. Then the two plantations could be worked side by side giving my sisters and I security for later.'

'Good God, he's not harping on that idea still, is he?'

Christie looked up startled. 'Grandmama?'

'Your Father's talked about that for years. Just because he and the Winthrops decided these things when you were babies. I thought he'd see sense now you are all older. What fools men are.'

'Grandmama, I don't understand.'

'Tell me this, girl. Are your sisters so ugly that they won't be married, then?'

'No, of course not. They are all quite attractive. Even little Carrie is pretty. Well, you have seen them for yourself.'

Her Grandmama sniffed, saying peevishly, 'When the minxes deign to visit me.' Then coming back to the subject, she continued: 'There you are, then. There will be no trouble in marrying them off so you don't have to worry about them. So it is just you we have to think about at the moment. How do you feel about this Joel?'

'That's just it, I hardly know him. But Papa is inviting him with Mr and Mrs Winthrop, to dine with us sometime soon.'

'M-mm. Well, you'll make up your own mind, no doubt. But from what I hear of the Winthrops I wouldn't be too eager to tie the knot, if I were you.'

'Really, Grandmama? Why not? Do you know Joel?'

'No, I don't. But I know of the family. But you will see Joel and decide for yourself. But remember this, Christie,' she placed her claw-like hand on Christie's. 'When you marry, choose who you want, do not marry to please your Father. I know Thomas, he always did get these damn foolhardy ideas in his head. My advice to you is to see this Joel but also go and meet other young people. See who else there is around. Don't you know any girls who have brothers, for instance?'

'No, not really. And since Mama died I haven't had time, you know.'

'Mm. Highly inconsiderate of your mother to go before she could have helped you.'

Shocked, Christie said, 'But poor Mama hardly died on purpose.'

'I know, but it was at a most inconvenient time for you girls. Well, you can't do more at the moment, I suppose. See this Joel by all means, but keep an open mind and meet some others if you can before making the big decision. So, there you are, child.' She gave Christie's hand a final squeeze. 'That's my advice to you.

Marry where your heart is and not to please anyone else. Not even your father. If he makes trouble, I'll deal with him.'

'Thank you. I can think much straighter now and I won't be hurried into making up my mind yet. I'll just take my time.' She kissed her Grandmama's cheek.

'Good, good. I'm tired now. I shall finish my smoke and then have a nap. Come and see me again and let me know what happens.'

'I will, I will,' smiled Christie. She kissed the wrinkled cheek once more and left with a much lighter step.

Later Zilpah, seeing how changed her young mistress was from the worried girl who had gone out that morning, shook her head. 'Dat Gran'ma is one clever lady,' she mused.

Chapter 4

The days came and went with the usual heat, routines of work, relaxation, chatter and laughter. Christie tried hard to find time to go out and visit friends again and to be brought up to date with the local gossip and news. Although she enjoyed a certain amount of this, a lot of it seemed a waste of time to her and she would have preferred to be doing something more useful.

After the initial panic of her impending courtship and subsequent marriage to Joel, Christie began to relax again. She had asked her father twice if he had had a reply to his letter regarding the prospective dinner they would give for the Winthrops but he had shaken his head with a not too pleased expression on his face, so Christie had said no more and had warned her sisters not to pester him or herself about the matter. The younger ones were disappointed as they had been looking forward to having new dresses for the occasion and had been busy sketching patterns and deciding colours.

However, it wasn't until the beginning of September, when the weather was a little more pleasant, that Thomas received a reply from Wilbur which he read out to the girls whilst at dinner one evening. He read:

Dear Thomas

Thank you for your most gracious letter inviting me, my wife and son to dinner one evening. I would like to accept this gracious invitation and hope the twentieth of the month will be convenient to you.

I have been away so that is why I haven't written earlier. I look forward to meeting you and your family, especially your eldest daughter.

Yours faithfully

Wilbur Winthrop

Charlotte and Carrie grinned and looked mischievously at Christie. Emma, noting Christie's pale face, tried to divert the attention away from her by remarking to her father, 'What an odd letter to be sure. Don't you think so, Papa? He doesn't say *we* would like to accept. Does that mean he will be the only one coming, do you think?'

Her father frowned. 'I shouldn't think so, Emma. It is a bit odd, I suppose, but I expect it's just his way of saying things.'

'May I see the letter, Papa?' asked Christie, recovering a little. Her father handed the letter over and watched her while she read it. 'Well?' he asked, a twinkle in his eye as she handed it back.

'It's not very scholarly. He's written "gracious" twice and he's tried to be friendly but finishes off like a business letter. Not very impressive.' She sniffed, began her dinner once more, decided she didn't want it now and pushed it away.

Her father smiled. 'Well, you will be able to show him how to write his letters in future, when you live there, won't you?'

'*If* I live there, Papa,' amended Christie.

'Christie?' Her papa frowned at her.

Christie, her face now pink, said determinedly, 'I might not want to live in Mrs Winthrop's house and she might not like me to. I should hope she has some say in the matter. Also, I haven't said "yes" to Joel's proposal yet, if he ever gets around to asking me, that is.'

Her father looked at her severely.

'But you know the agreement I had, Christie.'

'Yes,' said Christie, 'but it wasn't my agreement. I am quite happy to know Joel, Papa, but I cannot promise anything until I've spoken to him, seen the house and—and everything else.' Her face suffused with red, her lips compressed, and she looked straight at her father. 'I'm sorry, Papa, I can't agree to something or to marry someone whom I don't know. You wouldn't expect me to, would you?'

'I hoped you would be a dutiful daughter.'

'I hope to be too, but I cannot promise on this occasion. I'm sorry. Excuse me.' She rose from the table and without another word left the room.

Thomas began to rise from his chair. He had rather a shocked expression on his face and he did not look too pleased. But again Emma saved the moment by saying quietly: 'Papa, she is all right. She will return in a moment. Just leave her?'

Her father sat down again. Emma had the power to do this. She didn't know it, but as far as Thomas was concerned, it was as if his wife had been speaking with the same reasonable, soft voice.

'Yes,' he gave Emma a smile. 'Yes, of course.'

Charlotte, thinking she should help out over the difficult situation, asked: 'Papa?'

'Mmm?'

'Are we allowed new dresses for the occasion?' She looked pleadingly at her father, at the same time giving Carrie an unladylike kick under the table.

'Ooh, yes, Papa.' Carrie took Charlotte's hint. 'Do say we may. What colour would you like me to have? A bright red one?' She held up her hair and rolled her eyes.

Charlotte grinned at her encouragingly. Thomas couldn't help but laugh at her. 'You may have a new dress, you minx, but not red. Something light and pretty.'

'Leave it to us,' said Emma. 'We will find something suitable.'

By this time, Christie was able to return. It had taken all her courage to stand up to her father but with visions of her grandmother supporting her she had been able to do it. She found she felt better for taking this stance as she had decided she couldn't and wouldn't enter into a marriage that seemed a disaster from the outset. Now she took some deep breaths to stop the trembling and waited until she could breathe properly again before returning to the dining room.

She sat down once more and helped herself to some grapes while the others told her about the new dresses they hoped to have.

'And you must have one too,' said Thomas to Christie, looking warily at her. Christie, recognising the olive branch her father extended, looked sunnily at him.

'Of course,' she said, briefly touching his hand. The crisis was over.

In the days that followed an air of excitement entered into the Farrell household. Charlotte and Carrie chattered and giggled more and Emma smiled quietly to herself as she went about her daily routine. Thomas wore a satisfied expression because everything was going according to plan so he indulged his daughters quite happily when asked for extra money to buy toiletries and fripperies. Even the servants seemed to catch something of the changed atmosphere and went around with a lighter step and smiles on their faces.

But Zilpah frowned. She watched Christie as she had said very little, a strained look on her pale face. When Christie came to see Zilpah and the other servants in the kitchen, she smiled and was considerate as usual but she seemed to have lost her sparkle. It was replaced by a certain tenseness.

One day, Zilpah managed to see Christie alone outside in the yard near the kitchen. 'Miss Christie, can I have a word wit' you please?'

'Mm? Oh, yes Zilpah, what is it?'

'You'm not de same, Miss Christie. You unhappy?'

Christie sighed. 'No—no, Zilpah, thank you. It's just that I seem to have a lot happening in the future and I don't know whether I shall like it. I suppose in one way I'm frightened.'

'Miss Christie, de trouble is yous tink too much. Not'ing's happened yet. Wait. Don't tink.'

'You're right, of course, but I can't seem to help it. Will I like Joel? Will he like me? What about his parents? Will I like living with them? And it goes on and on.'

'It natural,' said Zilpah nodding. 'But you should wait and see. Someting will happen which will tell you if tings are good or bad. Den you decide.'

'I suppose so.'

'I know so. So come on, forget dat and tell me what we do to feed all dese people dat are coming to dinner.'

'There will only be eight of us, Zilpah,' smiled Christie.

'Dat's better, old Zilpah made you smile.'

'You're a great comfort, did you know that?' said Christie seriously.

'Huh-uh. The food, Miss Christie.'

'Well, let us see. How about shrimps and oysters cooked with butter, cream and egg yolks that Mama used to like so much?'

Zilpah nodded. 'And pieces of chicken with mushrooms and herbs?'

'Yes, that is good. Perhaps some other meat and the soufflé of sweet potatoes with sherry, also a selection of vegetables and okra soup? Then, shall we have some fruit tarts and rose and fruit salads? And anything else you like, Zilpah. Some of your different dishes with spices might be pleasant.'

Zilpah nodded. 'I do nice dinner. Don't worry.'

'Papa will see to the wines, I expect. Thank you, Zilpah. I don't know what we would do without you.' Christie smiled as she placed her hand on Zilpah's arm.

'Uh-huh,' grunted Zilpah.

Eventually Wednesday the twentieth arrived. There was extra work to be done and the servants with dusters, mops and polish cleaned the large dining room, which was used only on special occasions, until it glowed. Then the silver candlesticks and dishes were rubbed until they shone, as were the wine goblets.

Later in the afternoon fresh flowers and fruit were arranged in the epergne and placed in the centre of the table. When the candles were lit a soft glow warmed the room making silver and glass sparkle as they caught the light.

Christie caught her breath. It all looked beautiful. This is how she remembered it looked when her mama held dinners here for her many friends. It seemed like old times again as Christie was always allowed to stay up later to take part. Now, she began to feel a lot happier. Zilpah was right. 'Don't think about what might happen, just wait and see,' she told herself.

She went in search of her father who was neatly dressed in black knee breeches and a black coat with silver braiding. When he saw Christie he smiled. 'You look lovely, dear,' he said and kissed her cheek.

She was dressed in midnight blue silk with cream lace round the neckline and cascading from her elbow length sleeves. Her underskirt was of the same blue but heavily quilted and scattered with cream pearls. She had tied her long, dark hair to the side so that it fell over her left shoulder, with a matching blue ribbon and more pearls.

Emma appeared next in a shell pink dress. With her fair hair and colouring 'she looked good enough to eat' her father told her. Then the younger ones came, Charlotte in primrose and white, Carrie in pale blue and white. They had managed to curl their hair into ringlets and had added flowers to match their dresses. All the young ladies carried fans.

'Well, well,' said Thomas, beaming, 'how beautiful you all look. Thank you, ladies. We should have invited more young men. We shall have to see what we can do in the future, won't we, Christie?'

'Ye-es,' said Christie, imagining herself in the role of a mother and chaperone for her younger sisters.

Then they heard the rattle of carriage wheels and the clip-clop of hooves so arranged themselves in the parlour to receive their guests.

It wasn't long before the doors opened and the Winthrops were announced. First Wilbur came in, a tall, heavy man dressed in a blue coat that looked rather too tight across his shoulders. His hair was grey and his dark eyes looked around keenly until they alighted on Christie. But he turned back to Thomas quickly, shook hands heartily, saying: 'Neighbours, but we see little of each other, Thomas. Never mind, we get together when it's important, don't we?'

Thomas merely said, 'My eldest daughter, Christie.'

Christie curtseyed and began to welcome them, but was interrupted by Wilbur's booming voice: 'Well, well, you are quite a young lady now. Last time I saw you, you were a little girl with your mother.'

'That must have been a long time ago, Mr Winthrop. Oh, these are my sisters, Emma, Charlotte and Caroline.'

As he passed on to them, Christie turned and looked into the eyes of Marie Winthrop. They looked—frightened? The face beneath was powdered and rouged. As Christie smiled at her and made her welcome, a sweet smile transformed Marie's face. Christie thought she must have been beautiful once.

'I've been looking forward to meeting you again,' Marie said gently. 'It is some time since we met and I miss your Mama so much. She was so kind to me.'

Christie made her known to her sisters, then turned to find Joel waiting for her. He was tall like his father, slimmer, of course, but he looked strong with broad shoulders. His eyes were dark, which now looked laughingly down into hers. His fair hair was tied back and his coat, fitting rather better than his father's, was of a deep claret colour with gold braiding. He bowed slightly. So Christie curtseyed. She was just going to say her welcome words once more when Joel interrupted, saying: 'There's no need to repeat those words again. Tell me why I haven't seen you or met you before, instead.'

Christie blushed. 'Well,' she said, 'we haven't been out among people a great deal since Mama died, you know.' Then, as he grinned lazily down at her she continued, 'Also, I have met you and seen you before when we visited, but you were too old and stuck up to notice me.'

Joel grinned even more as she said this. 'Ah—ha, the kitten has claws, has she?'

'I'm sorry if I sounded rude, but...'

'Don't apologise, it's probably true. So how do you entertain yourself?'

'Well,' Christie smiled, 'it's not very exciting, I'm afraid, but I enjoy what I do mainly. I see to the running of the house and try and keep everyone happy. I help with the welfare of our workers too, as Papa is too busy to attend to that side of things. I visit friends and Grandmama and...'

'Life is full of entertainment for you, isn't it?'

'All right. If you don't think I have much fun, what do you do?'

'Would you like to know?' She nodded. 'But I don't think you would really, you know.'

They were interrupted by a black servant holding a tray of glasses of sherry. Christie took one off the tray, saying quietly: 'Thank you, Jonah. What are my younger sisters drinking?'

'It's all right, Miss Christie,' he grinned. 'I put lemonade in de sherry glasses for dem.'

Christie smiled back and nodded. 'Thank you.'

Joel had taken a glass, watching Christie. When Jonah had moved on, he asked, 'Why are you on such good terms with a slave?'

Christie thought it a funny question but said: 'He is a servant and has been with us a long time. He's good.'

'In what way?' Joel lifted an eyebrow.

Christie frowned, puzzled. 'He's good at his job, reliable, no trouble. Why do you ask? If he wasn't we wouldn't have him. Do you have good servants?'

Joel shrugged. 'I don't know about such things. The blacks look all alike to me but I recognise the difference between the men and the women. But it's my mother's work to attend to the matter of servants. We don't have many and they're white anyway.'

Christie thought this odd but said no more.

'So,' Joel went on, 'what are we going to do to put some excitement into your life?'

'Suggest something,' said Christie, her blue eyes twinkling.

'Well, let's see. There are some social events in town in an evening, now the weather is cooler, dances, the theatre and such things. And I can take you riding if you would like and we can visit the parks and gardens. We could take a boat on the river and walk round the shops. How am I doing?' Joel raised an enquiring eyebrow.

'Quite well,' said Christie, making her mouth prim. 'Please continue.'

'Thank you. We can walk by the river, take a trip…'

'You have already said we could take a trip on the river.'

'In the carriage, I was going to say when you interrupted.'

'And who would you like me to bring with me on all these jaunts? A servant or Emma?'

He made a face. 'Do we have to have someone?'

Christie opened her eyes wide. 'But of course we do. It would seem very odd for me not to have a chaperone of some kind.'

'Oh well, it had better be Emma, then.' He glanced in Emma's direction. 'Does she always look, er—sugary?'

'Emma,' said Christie fondly, 'has always been pretty. She takes after Mama, you know. And Papa often takes her advice, just like he did Mama's. She isn't stupid.'

'You've convinced me. Emma it must be.'

Christie took a much-needed sip of her sherry, noticing her father was talking to Mr Winthrop while the girls surrounded his wife. She seemed to be enjoying their company. Looking at her, Christie had the impression she wasn't a very happy lady and wondered why. Surely her situation compared favourably with theirs? The house was large and she thought the cotton fields were of a similar size. Then she looked at Mr Winthrop. Perhaps he was the trouble in some way. He was pleasant enough at the moment but Christie wondered if he was making an extra effort being in their company. He seemed very jolly, slightly boisterous and that in a large gentleman could be unnerving. She wouldn't be surprised that he had a quick temper, too. Was Joel the same, she wondered?

She looked up to find Joel's mocking eyes upon her. She found him rather difficult to deal with and hoped she was giving the right impression. He was looking slightly amused. He took another glass of sherry and said, 'So, what do you think?'

Christie looked up at him speculatively. 'Mm. I'll tell you some other time,' she said quietly.

'I'm all a-quake. Are you always so serious?'

Fortunately Christie was saved from replying by the doors opening and dinner being announced.

'Mrs Winthrop, may I take you into dinner?' Thomas asked. She rose, smiling, and placed a hand on his arm.

Mr Winthrop came over to Christie. 'Mine must be the pleasure, my dear,' he said. So Christie followed on Wilbur's arm, leaving Joel who said, with an exaggerated sigh, 'So I must escort the, er—luscious Emma.'

As there were no more gentlemen to partner the two younger sisters, Charlotte said in a deep voice to Carrie: 'Miss Farrell, will you do me the honour?'

So Carrie, making a prim face and placing her hand on Charlotte's arm, murmured: 'A pleasure, I'm sure.' So with straight backs and heads held high they proceeded to follow the others to the dining room, biting their lips hard to stop themselves from giggling.

CHAPTER 5

▼

The dining room was just as it should be. The candles sent warm glows around the room and on to the feast that reposed on the long oak dining table. Zilpah and her minions had spared no effort to set before them the most beautifully cooked food and tasty dishes. Smartly dressed servants waited in the shadows ready to serve the diners.

Thomas sat at the head of the table with Christie the opposite end as his hostess. Beside him, Mrs Winthrop remarked quietly with a smile how wonderful everything looked. Charlotte, sitting opposite, gave her a broad grin. Christie, with Mr Winthrop on her right and Joel on her left, felt a little overpowered with two almost unknown men beside her. Then a picture of her Grandmama came to mind, so she took a deep breath and straightened her back, determined to take charge of the situation as hostess.

Unfortunately, things began badly. Mr Winthrop, trying to be a sociable guest, picked up a dish of spiced stewed meat to offer to Christie. It was too hot for his fingers and he managed to spill some of it on to the cloth. He went rather red in the face and, looking round, found everyone else waiting quietly for Thomas to say grace. So with a hurried bow of the head and hands in his lap he became even more embarrassed. Or was he angry? Christie wondered.

Grace having been said, the servants moved forward, two to serve the wine, two to serve the food. One hastily mopped up the spillage that had been made. Christie, thinking she must now ignore the incident completely, tried to think of a topic of conversation that would please both her male guests. She succeeded by asking if Mr Winthrop attended any social functions in town and had he met any of her family's acquaintances, possibly at the music soirees or the literary meetings. Joel interrupted to say they attended other events.

'Oh,' said Christie, 'and what would those be?'

'Where only men are allowed to go, my dear.'

'Why?'

Before Joel could answer his father interrupted. 'We like to play cards and games the ladies wouldn't like.'

'Oh,' said Christie. She felt it a poor answer and when she looked at Joel's mocking face knew it was time to introduce a new topic of conversation. So during the rest of the meal she thought of subjects like the weather, the new buildings in town and the price of cigars. The conversation flowed pleasantly enough.

Christie noticed Mrs Winthrop seemed to be really enjoying herself and was chattering happily to Emma and Thomas. She was most gracious towards the servants when served with food or wine, following Thomas's and the girls' examples. So why didn't Joel and Mr Winthrop do the same? When they needed more wine they just held up their goblets until they were filled again, with no word of thanks. Jonah, being one of the wine servers, looked once to Christie for her approval to keep filling up the goblets. She nodded, saying pointedly, 'Thank you, Jonah,' but her example wasn't followed.

Eventually, everyone's appetite satiated, Christie stood up to lead the ladies to the withdrawing room, while the men drank their port, discussed manly topics and relieved themselves.

The young ladies clustered round Mrs Winthrop as she smilingly looked at all their pretty faces. Christie had the impression she was enjoying herself hugely.

'You must all come and visit me,' she said. 'I'm afraid our house isn't as grand as this one but it would be lovely for me if you could visit sometimes.' She placed a thin hand over Christie's. 'And you must come and stay a while when you get to know Joel better. I would enjoy your company so much, my dear.'

So Christie smiled, wondering if the feeling could be reciprocated. She quite liked Mrs Winthrop but felt more sorry for her than anything else. If she was to be her future mama-in-law, did she expect Christie to be like a daughter and be with her for company? Christie didn't feel too impressed with the idea.

It wasn't long before the gentlemen returned, Mr Winthrop rubbing his hands and saying, 'A lovely meal, wonderful.' The talk was general for a while, then Joel took a pack of cards from his pocket. 'Come along, all you lovely young ladies, I am going to show you a trick.' So he amused them by expertly dealing out the cards, asking them to guess where 'the lady' was, meaning the Queen of Hearts, and confusing them with his sleight of hand and artifice. He knew many tricks and Charlotte and Carrie thought how wonderful and clever it all was. Christie tried to enter into the spirit of it all but kept glancing at her father to see if he approved. She didn't think he did, but he said nothing, only smiling at their indignant faces when they hadn't found the solution to the puzzle.

By now it was late and the Winthrops decided to depart. As they all were saying their farewells, Joel took Christie's hands. 'It was a lovely evening,' he said. 'Shall I call for you tomorrow morning about eleven o'clock? Why don't you bring all your sisters and then perhaps we can manage to escape from them for a few minutes?' He smiled down into Christie's eyes.

'Very well,' was all Christie said. 'I shall look forward to it.' He pulled her towards him and kissed her cheek, then turned, shook hands with Thomas, called a general 'goodnight' and left.

'Now, my children, up to bed,' Thomas Farrell smiled. 'Thank you all for your contributions to tonight. I was proud of you all. I think it went very well.' He looked at Christie. 'We'll speak tomorrow, after breakfast.'

'Yes, Papa. Oh! Joel is coming to take us all out at eleven o'clock. You will all be there, won't you?' she asked them all rather anxiously.

'How wonderful,' breathed Charlotte, her eyes shining.

In bed that night, Christie wondered if she would ever go to sleep. She had enjoyed the meal and she was pleased with herself and her sisters' behaviour. She wasn't too impressed by Mr Winthrop, though. He seemed to her to be more at home with other men rather than ladies. He certainly lacked charm. She wondered why Mrs Winthrop had agreed to marry him in the first place. She seemed so different but perhaps he was like Joel when young, attractive with a certain charm. Did that mean Joel would be like his father as he became older? The prospect wasn't a very pleasant thought. It was rather pathetic hearing Mrs Winthrop asking the girls to visit. Had she no friends of her own? She must be a lonely lady but Christie felt she didn't want to be the one to remedy that loneliness.

Then there was Joel. Did she like him? Although there was much she didn't like, perhaps that could be altered? If he behaved less like his father, he would be better. Charlotte and Carrie certainly enjoyed his company and from Christie's point of view it was nice to be singled out and kissed. It made her feel special and warm inside. So perhaps that was proof that she quite liked Joel, really? Still, she was pleased her sisters were invited out tomorrow. And so her thoughts went round and round in her head. It was over an hour later before she finally drifted off to sleep.

The following day they were at breakfast as usual, Charlotte and Carrie extolling Joel's virtues and looking forward to their trip out later that morning.

'Did you like him?' asked Carrie eagerly. 'Did he kiss you?'

'Really, dear, you shouldn't ask those things,' Emma rebuked her sister mildly.

'Well, I think he is wonderful. I said he's handsome, and he is. You are lucky, Christie.'

Christie shrugged, trying to be cool and calm in an effort to stop her heart from beating faster. 'We shall see,' was all she would say.

After breakfast she found her father in his study. 'Come in, my dear and tell me your opinions on last evening. I thought the meal was excellent and I've already sent our thanks to Zilpah.'

'Oh, yes, Zilpah promised it would be good. I thought Mrs Winthrop rather a pathetic figure. Her dress wasn't new, you know, neither was Mr Winthrop's coat. It was much too tight for him. I feel he is overbearing and his wife receives the brunt of it.'

'Do you mean he's cruel?'

'As to that I don't know, but I wouldn't like to be alone with him for any length of time. I don't think I could trust him.'

'And Joel?'

'Well, certainly the girls enjoyed his company. I suppose I did but I'm not really sure, yet. Time will tell, won't it?'

'Oh, yes, well,' answered Thomas disappointedly, then with a shrug continued, 'At least you don't say you can't stand the sight of him. Perhaps after a week or two you'll feel differently,' he finished hopefully.

Later that morning Joel arrived as promised and sat between Charlotte and Carrie in the carriage opposite to Christie and Emma. He didn't seem any worse for his late night and Christie thought waspishly that he was probably used to it. Then she silently raked herself down for thinking such unkind thoughts about him. He seemed to be quite happy to be the only man among four young ladies and she wondered whether he really enjoyed it or whether he was being kind. She did notice he kept looking at her and wondered why. She came to the conclusion he was just trying to make her feel uncomfortable for devilment, so glared back at him. His smile broadened. She ignored him and pointedly turned to talk to Emma, commenting on the scenery.

Eventually Joel called for the driver to stop so that they could walk amongst the flowering bushes and trees where it was cool. Emma took charge of the younger girls and walked in one direction, while Joel, taking Christie by the hand, walked in the opposite direction. They were quiet for a while and Christie thought how relaxing and pleasant it all was. Then Joel broke the silence.

'And why did I have to be glared at?' he smiled.

Christie looked up at him. 'Because you were staring at me.'

'Don't you like being stared at?'

'No, it's rude.'

'I thought it very pleasant.' Christie had the grace to blush while Joel went on, 'Can you guess what I was thinking?'

She shook her head. 'No, I don't want to.'

He ignored her and went on: 'I was wondering what you'd look like without your clothes on.'

She stopped and turned, an incredulous look in her blue eyes. Then anger took its place. 'Don't you dare speak to me like that again!' she cried.

Joel grinned. 'We shall deal with one another famously,' he said, taking her into his arms and kissing her. She struggled, but as he was larger and stronger than she was, she was soon overpowered. After what seemed a long time, when her breathing became laboured, he let her go. Although she felt weak from the different emotions she was experiencing, anger came to the forefront and she found the energy to give him a sharp slap across his face. Then she ran as fast as she could towards the waiting carriage. Joel followed quickly, annoyed with himself for thinking she was ready for 'playing games' and more annoyed with Christie for having the audacity to hit him.

The scene he then saw when he came up to the carriage did little to mollify him. He found not only Emma and the girls were partaking of lemonade, but the black servant as well. Even the horse had been given water to drink.

'What is all this?' asked Joel testily.

Emma said: 'Oh, do have a drink, Joel. We thought it a good idea.'

'Thank you, but I don't drink with servants.'

Emma looked unhappy. 'I'm sorry,' she faltered.

Christie by now had recovered her composure. 'I'm afraid you will have to get used to us, Joel. We always treat our servants fairly as far as we are able. And our horses.'

There was an uncomfortable silence while Christie seated herself in the carriage once more. Now Carrie, with great daring said, 'Everyone has finished, Joel. Would you like a drink now?'

'Thank you,' he said, taking the proffered glass. Carrie smiled.

On the return journey everyone was rather quiet, not knowing what one another were thinking. But eventually small talk was resumed until Farrell Hall was reached. The girls, apart from Christie, thanked Joel for the trip and went off into the house.

'All right,' said Joel after they had gone, 'I was wrong and I'm sorry.'

Christie's face lightened. 'Thank you, Joel,' she said gently. 'Let's forget it.'
'Can I take you out again? I'll behave, I promise.'
'Of course,' said Christie. 'I'll just bring Emma next time.'

Later, Christie congratulated herself. She felt she had taught Joel a lesson and in future he would behave with a little more decorum. He would realise she wasn't just a silly little miss to behave with as he chose and he would learn to mind her in time. She thought he could be a lot of fun and quite charming if only he would put his mind to it. She sighed. She would have to see what she could do to alter him. But all things considered, everything seemed to be going well.

Christie would not have felt so comfortable with herself if she had seen Joel as he returned home. He felt quite differently. He stormed into the house, a grim look on his face. For all his repentance in front of Christie he now cursed himself for being so weak. 'Silly little bitch,' he muttered, 'who does she think she is?' Unfortunately there was a china vase standing on the hall table. He picked it up and threw it at the wall. There was an ear splitting crash. His father's voice boomed out from the study on the right.

'Joel, come in!'

Joel, exasperated with everybody and everything in general, opened the door and stalked into his father's presence leaving the door to bang and close itself. He collapsed onto the nearest chair without a word of greeting, not waiting for permission from his father.

Wilbur looked at him, noting the signs of antagonism but said with an attempt at jollity, 'Well, how did it go?'

'She didn't like being kissed and smacked my face.' Joel glowered at his father, his face like a thundercloud.

Wilbur laughed. 'Oho, she has spirit, has she? I did wonder. Come on, boy, you'll have great fun with her.'

Joel looked at him with dislike. 'Do I have to go on with this? It's not as if I like the girl really, or any of the Farrells. The girls are not up to snuff and have no idea of fun. The best of the lot is Carrie but she's only fourteen. Christie's not going to be easy and I don't see why I have to be shackled with the girl just because you and her father decided a long time ago that it was a good idea.'

Wilbur interrupted. 'Now look here, my son. Thomas has always thought that an amalgamation of the two properties by you marrying his daughter was a sensible thing to do. He has always held that ridiculous notion. But that's not what's at stake any more, is it? We must have money and Christie's dowry is one way of getting it. Thomas will be generous I feel sure, especially as it culminates in a project dear to his heart. But…'—and here he thumped on his desk with his fist to emphasise every word, 'we must have money. You gamble and fritter away every amount you can lay your hands on. Now it's up to you to restore, in part, some of our family fortune. I don't think it too much to ask, do you?'

'Oh, and I suppose you don't gamble either?' Joel answered bitterly, curling his lip. 'Who took me out and showed me how? And for that matter, who introduced me to certain ladies…?'

'Yes, yes, I know. But that's what men do!'

'All right, I grant you that's all entertaining, but now you expect me to act like a saint.'

'Well, it's not all my fault. We lost money on the cotton last year because of the bol weevil, and the slaves I sold didn't bring in much. I can't sell any more, otherwise there won't be enough to pick the cotton. Listen, boy, all you have to do is act the pretty for a week or two, then we'll invite Christie to come and stay for a while. It's not as if you have to be with her all day, just an hour or two here and there. You can make some excuses. You can say you have to supervise the slaves or you have work to do. She will be with your mother most of the time, anyway. I'll tell your mother to keep Christie with her. Ladies like to chat, look at magazines and go out in the carriage. Once you're married you can be as free from her as you wish. She will be too busy with the babies, won't she?' Wilbur laughed, pointing a finger towards his son. 'Come on, boy, how about it?'

Chapter 6

The weather became cooler and therefore more pleasant, enabling social activities in the town to begin once more in earnest. There were interesting lectures about new flowers that had been discovered; also, people who had travelled to other countries came to tell of their experiences, showing drawings of birds and animals that had never been seen before. There were musical concerts with singers and sometimes recitations, parties, invitations to dinners and balls.

The Farrell girls, now no longer in mourning, took the opportunity to attend as many of the various functions as possible. Here they met old acquaintances, were introduced to new ones and generally enjoyed themselves. Carrie, especially, was in a fever of excitement, as this was her first season attending such things. Her older sisters made sure they kept a watchful eye on her. Of course, new dresses had to be made, new shoes bought and such things as gloves, fichus, fans and jewellery, although the latter could be borrowed from one's sisters. Sometimes this ended in squabbles, which Emma, with her quiet manner and soft voice, was usually able to sort out. Thomas, if not out of the house, usually shut himself in his study on such occasions.

The work at home still had to continue, however, and now Christie was often out with Joel, Charlotte had to take over more of her tasks. But with her sunny disposition and boundless energy, she just accepted this quite happily and made a good effort, particularly in visiting the workers and looking after their welfare.

Christie, of course, was supposed to be enjoying Joel's company and her outings with him. She met him at some social events but as there was no official engagement he could not be with her all the time. So she would only stand up with him for two of the dances as propriety dictated and the rest of the time she had no knowledge of where he was.

On certain mornings he would call for her and they would go in to Charleston by carriage or walk by the river. If she asked him if he was happy doing these things he would turn to her, looking as though his mind was elsewhere. Then, as she looked earnestly at him, he would grin, saying: 'It's fun, isn't it?' Sometimes he treated her quite offhandedly, as though they were strangers and Christie felt that their knowledge of each other was not progressing as it should. When she saw him, her heart beat faster, and she admitted to herself she was attracted by his good looks—but wasn't there supposed to be a deeper feeling for each other, somehow? Was she really in love with him, she wondered? How did she know?

One day, for a change, she suggested they should go riding. Christie was a good rider and had learnt from an early age. So one morning Joel rode over on a large showy horse. Christie had dressed in a very fetching habit of blue just a fraction deeper than her eyes and she looked particularly pretty that morning. Her chestnut mare was ready and they set off at a walk until they reached open countryside. Without a word Joel put his horse to the gallop. Did he expect her to follow or was he trying to impress her? He had been very quiet that morning. Was he bored? Blowed if she knew. She didn't know what to make of him. Perhaps he was moody? But she thought if he rode in that neck or nothing fashion, sooner or later he would have an accident. So she galloped carefully, meeting him as he turned back towards her.

'That feels better!' he called out to her.

'I don't think you should ride like that, Joel. You could come off, you know, and the horse might have caught his foot…'

'Don't be so bloody bossy, Christie. I ride well so don't try and tell me otherwise.'

Instead of feeling chastened, much to Joel's annoyance, Christie said quite placidly, 'We shall see then, won't we?'

She began to ride forward again, hoping he had calmed down. He looked like a spoilt boy so perhaps that was the problem. As he was the youngest, had he been spoilt? He continued to ride in silence. Christie thought it was up to her to make the next move. She moved her horse alongside and said without preamble: 'Joel, I apologise. It was rude of me to say what I did. It comes of my being the eldest, I suppose.' She looked at him and was relieved to see a kind of smile on his face. 'I'll race you back,' was all he said. Christie thought it best to let him win.

They dismounted and led their horses towards the house. As Christie was speaking, a figure came running over the lawn. It was Joseph.

'Is he supposed to be there?' asked Joel, a frown on his face. 'Shall I get rid of him for you?' He handled his whip suggestively.

'Certainly not,' said Christie. 'If Joseph is coming over the lawn there is something wrong. What is it, Joseph?' she called.

Joseph, by now out of breath, managed to say, 'Sorry, Miss Christie. One of de children is very sick.'

'Right,' said Christie, 'take my horse to Jacob and tell him to fetch the doctor right away. Then ask Zilpah for a drink.'

'Yes, Miss Christie. Thank you. Thank you, sir.'

'I'm sorry, Joel. I must go as you can see.'

'Must you?' Joel looked puzzled.

'Yes, you see a child needs help. I must check if Papa is home or perhaps you can do that for me and then I can…'

But she was interrupted. 'No, no,' said Joel. 'He won't want to be bothered with me. I'll just go.' He climbed on to his horse's back and was gone.

It wasn't until later when they were all seated together after dinner, that Christie remembered Joel's words. She had had a busy time as no one had been at home to help. She had gone with Joseph to see the little girl and await the doctor. He pronounced a fever, gave instructions to the mother and left medicine to ease the condition. Hopefully, the child would be well again in a few days' time. Christie decided that Joel would not help with anything to do with slaves. She wondered how his own fared and hoped his mother was more tolerant. But why hadn't he wanted to see her father? If she and Joel were to be married, surely this would have been a good time to know him better? She thought over the day they had had and came to the conclusion that she knew Joel even less than when they had first gone out together. She felt she had done her best, but if he was going to be as difficult when they were married, it wasn't going to be a very happy union. She would like to have discussed it all with her Grandmama, but she was visiting her daughter for a while and was away from home. So there was nothing else for it—she must tell her father.

Carrie broke into her thoughts. She sang: 'Christie's thinking of Jo-el, Christie's thinking…'

'That will do, Carrie,' said her father. 'Christie's had a hard day and is probably tired. Isn't that so, Christie?'

'Mmm? Oh, yes, yes. I suppose so. Could I speak to you, Papa, do you think? In private, I mean?'

'Of course. Come along into the study. I wanted to speak to you anyway but I was leaving it until the morning as you looked so tired.'

'Thank you. But why do you wish to see me?'

'I've had a letter from Joel's parents inviting you to go and stay next week. Things are going well, hey?' He rubbed his hands together. 'So you will prepare yourself for the visit?'

'You've had a letter? Joel didn't say anything today. I wonder why?'

'Well,' her father grinned, 'perhaps he doesn't know and it's going to be a big surprise for him.'

'I'm sure it will be,' said Christie thoughtfully.

'So, I can answer it and say you'll be pleased to go? Good. Now, what was it you wanted to speak to me about?'

'It—it wasn't important, really. And I am rather tired as you said. I think bed is the best thing for me right now.'

'You are pleased to be going to Wilbur's, dear, aren't you?'

'Yes, of course. It's just that I'm tired.' She gave him what she hoped was a reassuring smile as she left, called in to say goodnight to her sisters and went wearily to her room.

She was brushing her hair when she heard a tap on her door.

'Who is it?'

'It's Emma. Can I come in for a moment?'

'Yes, of course. Is there a problem, dear?'

Emma closed the door and went and sat on the bed. 'I think you should tell me that. I don't wish to pry, Christie, but are you really happy with Joel? Recently, you've looked so worried and pale. Can I help? If you'd rather I went away, just say so.'

'Well, you see, I don't seem to be getting any further with Joel and, quite honestly, I just don't understand him. I was going to tell Papa just now that I really didn't think I could go through with it all but he's had a letter inviting me to stay with the Winthrops next week. He was so pleased about it. I didn't like to tell him how I felt.'

'I could tell something was wrong. What are you going to do?'

'I shall have to go and I might find things different there, of course. Joel might seem better in his own home.' She fiddled with the hairs on her brush while she said this.

'Well,' said Emma, trying to think of something that would cheer Christie up, 'how would it be if, after a day or two, I came and visited you and Mrs Winthrop? Then another day I'll send Charlotte and Carrie. After all, they said they would visit when the Winthrops were dining here.'

'Oh, Em, *would* you?' asked Christie, looking up quickly, a smile on her face. 'You see, none of us have been away from home on our own before, have we? Of course, it could be fun and I might enjoy it all. Thank you, Em.' She kissed her sister fondly, feeling happier for her visit and suggestions.

The following week saw Christie feverishly trying to prepare for her impending stay with the Winthrops. She had cotton dresses washed, silk dresses hung out in the air and a new one made for a special evening. She thought that she and Joel might be invited to a ball or that a similar occasion might be arranged for her. Emma helped her to choose her jewellery and then to pack. So by the Sunday afternoon, after attending church in the morning and having a last lunch with the family, Jacob brought the carriage round. With an understanding nod from Emma, smiles and waves from the girls and a jovial laugh from her father, she was soon on her way. She had seen Zilpah in the morning who had put her arms round her and given her a hug. 'If you's not happy, come home, huh?' Christie had smiled and nodded through gathering tears. Good gracious, anyone would think she was going to another country instead of a few miles along the road!

Christie arrived at the Winthrops' house, which was not as large as Farrell Hall but even so, it was bigger than some plantation houses. Jacob stopped outside the front door and Christie alighted. There was no sign of life so she climbed the steps to the front door and rang the bell. Eventually, a servant opened the door saying: 'Yes?'

Christie said: 'I'm Miss Farrell come to stay. Could someone bring in my baggage, please?'

The servant looked past her, then turned without a word and disappeared through a doorway at the back of the hall, leaving her standing.

She went inside and waited again for about ten minutes before the man came back with another. Without a word they both went outside while Christie still stood. She looked round and saw that the hall was dark and felt cool but there were no welcoming vases of flowers or attractive paintings on the walls as at the Hall, but she supposed these things were not to everyone's taste. When her baggage had been brought, she noticed that Jacob had departed and she felt very much alone.

'Could Mrs Winthrop be told I've arrived?' she asked.

The men looked at each other. Then without a word they went back to what was presumably the servants' quarters. After another considerable wait a woman appeared who looked to be the housekeeper. Christie noticed that the servants were white and then remembered Joel's words.

'Oh, Miss. I can't tell Mrs Winthrop you're here, she's resting,' said the woman. She was obviously flustered. 'You weren't expected until next week,' she said.

'The date in the letter was today's date,' said Christie firmly. 'And if Mrs Winthrop cannot be fetched, perhaps either of the Mr Winthrops could?'

'But I don't know where they are, Miss,' said the woman, looking puzzled.

Fortunately, just at that precise moment, Joel came into the hall dressed ready for riding. He saw Christie and said, 'What are you doing here?'

'Well, really!' Christie was angry. 'I have come here because I was invited and no one seems to know anything about it. If I'm not supposed to be here, please order the carriage and I'll go back home again.'

Joel looked confused. 'I expect my father wrote and forgot to tell anybody,' he said by way of explanation. To the housekeeper he said, 'Ask my mother to come down.'

'But…' she began.

'Get her!' He turned with a snarl and the housekeeper fled. 'She will be here in a few moments and then everything will be all right. I'm afraid I have an appointment, otherwise…'

'Oh, please don't let me hold you up,' Christie said sarcastically, but Joel didn't seem to notice.

'Fine,' he said. 'Why don't you wait in the room over there? My mother won't be long.' And with a cheery whistle he left Christie standing.

She went to the room Joel had indicated and sat down on one of the straight-backed chairs. Here again the room was cheerless and she wondered if it was ever used. By the look of it, it could do with a good polish and the windows flung open, she thought. She waited a considerable time but eventually the door opened and Marie Winthrop entered. She looked as though she had just woken up from a deep sleep, which indeed she had. Christie stood up.

'Christie, how nice of you to come,' Marie said.

Christie, noting her dishevelled appearance, said: 'I beg your pardon but I believe I must have disturbed you. Are you ill, Mrs Winthrop?'

'No, no dear, it's just that I have taken something the doctor gave me to make me sleep. But I'm all right.' She tottered forward and sat on a chair.

'I'm sorry,' said Christie, 'but the date in the letter Papa received from Mr Winthrop was today's, but it seems it was the wrong date. If you like I can return home.'

'Oh, no, no. If my husband wrote it must be right. Come with me into my sitting room, it is much pleasanter and I will ask someone to prepare your room.'

The sitting room was much lighter and had some pretty drapes at the windows decorated with pink rosebuds and covered chairs to match. The furniture was old and rather heavy but there were some pretty pictures on the walls and china on the mantelpiece. After they were seated Marie apologised profusely again for the unfortunate welcome they had given Christie but, she vowed, they would all make it up to her and hoped she would have a happy stay with them.

Christie felt sorry for Mrs Winthrop as she was genuinely upset about Christie's reception. This had the effect of calming Christie down, enabling her to reply more kindly to Mrs Winthrop's questions and chatter. After about an hour, a knock came on the door and the housekeeper entered.

'Miss's room is ready now,' she said. 'Shall I show you the way?'

Christie jumped up. 'Thank you,' she said.

'Yes, yes, do go with Cooper, dear. Have you a key for Miss Farrell?'

'No, but I can find her one.'

'I think it would be wise,' said Marie, looking at Mrs Cooper and nodding. 'Keep your door locked at all times,' she added, looking at Christie. 'And take your key with you wherever you go. We don't want the—the servants, er...do we?' She left the question for Christie to make of what she would. Mrs Cooper sniffed.

Christie's room was pleasant with a view of a stretch of lawn from the window. Here again the furniture was dark and heavy but the bed looked comfortable and all was clean.

'Shall I help you unpack?' asked Mrs Cooper. She didn't sound too eager to help but at least she had offered.

'Oh, no, thank you. I'm sure you've a lot of other things to do. I can manage. How many girls are employed in the house?' Christie asked with a smile.

'Girls, Miss?' Mrs Cooper looked startled.

'Servants.'

'Oh, I see. Well, we don't have any. We have a woman who comes in to clean and do the washing. But otherwise there's just me and the two men you saw.'

'Good gracious,' Christie stared at her. 'How do you manage? You cook the food as well then?'

'That's right, Miss.'

'Then I'm sorry you have been put to so much trouble on my account.'

'Thank you, Miss, but it has all been done, so there's nothing to worry about. I'll find you a key for your room.' She even smiled as she left.

Christie thought it strange that there were no servants, but Mrs Cooper seemed an agreeable enough person if treated properly. Evidently the Winthrops 'did' for themselves. How strange. She wondered what other differences there were.

The meal that evening, although of plain fare, was good and tasty and well cooked. Mr Winthrop hardly apologised for his lapse of memory in informing others of Christie's arrival but he excused himself by saying he was a very busy man with much to do. Joel said nothing at the time apart from raising an eyebrow. Mrs Winthrop looked slightly better than previously and chattered away to Christie. Afterwards, Joel was much more relaxed and teased Christie on being so serious. Finally he encouraged her to play cards with him and said later it had been a pleasure to teach her. In fact, she had enjoyed being with him and learning something different. It had been a gambling game but he said there was no harm if they played only for counters and not money.

As she lay in her bed that night, Christie thought what a complex character Joel was. Nothing could have been nicer than his attention that evening. He seemed a different person to the one she encountered when she arrived. If only he was as attentive like that more often. She felt she could like him very well if he was. She snuggled down with a happy feeling inside her and she hoped that on the next day they could have a trip out together somewhere. There was a limit to how much one could enjoy the company of Marie Winthrop!

Chapter 7

▼

Christie slept well and was up and awaiting her breakfast at her usual early hour. Mrs Cooper was surprised to see her but she quietly set an adequate breakfast of toast, preserves and coffee before her. As Christie sat down she tried to have a conversation with the housekeeper but she tried in vain as Mrs Cooper answered only in monosyllables while she seemed to be listening for something. For what, Christie wondered? When she elicited the fact that Joel and his father were still abed and that Mrs Winthrop would not appear until later either, it was obvious that Mrs Cooper was on edge. Perhaps she had to place their meal in front of them as soon as they came down, at whatever time that was, or she was in trouble, Christie mused. She wondered how anyone could keep a large house, servants and the cotton field workers well organised without some show of presence, especially first thing in the morning. And that was another thing: no one had told her yet about the slaves they had and whereabouts they lived. When did Mrs Winthrop visit them? It was early days yet, of course, she wouldn't be given information about everything all at once, but she intended to find out. If she was supposed to be marrying into this family she wanted to know what her place in it would be. Perhaps when she was out with Joel later that morning she could broach the subject.

This idea, however, never came to fruition as Mrs Winthrop came down to breakfast earlier than usual, according to Mrs Cooper's remarks, and before her husband. She told Christie she hoped she would go shopping with her that morning in Charleston. They would have a delightful time and take the carriage. So Christie had no option but to smile and acquiesce. Perhaps Mrs Winthrop looked forward to buying some clothes in which she would like Christie's opinion? She must find it difficult to shop alone, although by the look of what she wore she hadn't bought anything new for some time. Perhaps she hoped for female company to give her encouragement, as she seemed quite a nervous person.

So they took the carriage, the driver being the same black servant Joel had brought when he had visited Farrell Hall. When he saw Christie his sullen features altered and the beginning of a smile appeared on his face. He even touched his hat to her. Christie smiled and said 'Good morning' and asked his name.

'Zak, Miss,' he answered.

Marie Winthrop looked at Christie in surprise but said nothing. They drove off and the first stop was the market. After a lot of looking, only a small bunch of flowers was bought by Marie, which she gave to Christie. She duly thanked her but hoped they wouldn't wilt too much before they arrived home. Then they took the carriage along further to the shops.

Marie's idea of shopping was to look at everything and buy nothing. At first Christie entered into the spirit of the outing and agreed or disagreed on what Mrs Winthrop said over the various materials or the merits of a certain powder or the quality of the gloves she handled, but after a while this began to pall and eventually Christie was bored—so much so that she could have screamed.

At the earliest opportunity she suggested they went and quenched their thirst with a refreshing drink in a little parlour not far away. Marie looked vaguely at her and said, 'Very well, dear.'

'Shall we say we'll need the carriage in an hour?' Christie asked.

'He'll wait, dear,' Marie answered.

'But he's sitting in the sun. He doesn't want to do that for an hour.' She opened her reticule and took out some money. 'Go and find a drink, Zak, but not alcohol, mind, and give the horse some water. Come back in an hour, please.'

'Oh, yes Miss, thank you Miss,' and Christie was rewarded with a large white grin.

Marie said: 'Really, dear, you shouldn't spend your money on servants, you know. We never do.'

'Perhaps they would be happier if you did,' Christie flashed back at her. Then she could have bitten her tongue out as Marie said: 'Oh dear,' and looked so anxious and worried, her fingers plucking at her dress distressfully.

When they had sat down with a glass each of a fresh lemon drink, Christie said: 'Tell me, Mrs Winthrop, how many servants do you have? I've seen Mrs Cooper and the two men who brought in my baggage and Zak, of course, but are there any others I don't know about?'

'No, no, they are all we need,' Marie spoke hurriedly. 'This lemon is good,' she said, trying to change the subject.

Christie wouldn't be fobbed off. If Joel couldn't talk to her or even see her she would have to find out what she wanted to know from Mrs Winthrop. So Christie ignored her and asked: 'When do you visit the slaves, Mrs Winthrop?'

Marie spluttered over her drink. She dabbed at her mouth with her handkerchief. 'Really, Christie, you shouldn't ask these things, especially as we are in here.' She vaguely waved her hand indicating the parlour. 'People will hear.'

Christie frowned. Mrs Winthrop might be her mama-in-law in the future but she wasn't going to take reprimands from her all the same. So she said: 'I don't see what's wrong in asking a simple question. I asked because the next time you visit them I'd like to go with you.'

'But I don't visit them.' Marie looked shocked. 'I never have. They are my husband's and Joel's responsibility.'

Christie opened her eyes wide. 'But how can they look after the women and children?' she asked.

'I don't know, don't ask me. Oh dear, perhaps we'd better go.' She dabbed at her lips, then fiddled with her reticule.

'We can't yet, Zak won't be ready. We told him to come back in an hour.'

'You see, you should have let him wait, you…'

Christie broke in. 'All right, all right, we'll talk of something else,' she soothed but she was now intrigued, wondering what all the fuss was about.

By the time they returned home Mr Winthrop and Joel were out and Marie said she must rest and suggested Christie did the same as they had had a strenuous morning. This was the last thing Christie wanted to do and said so but added that she could amuse herself. So she went to find Mrs Cooper in the servants' quarter.

'Oh, Miss, you shouldn't be down here,' said Mrs Cooper, aghast.

'Now let me get this straight,' Christie said. 'Is it you who doesn't want me down here, or are you frightened that Mr Winthrop would object? If you don't like me to be here, I will go away, but if it's because of….'

She didn't get any further. Mrs Cooper was nodding. 'Yes, Miss, he wouldn't like you to be down here.'

'Well, he won't know, will he? If he does find out I'll deal with him. Now, could I sit with you and have some lunch please? Anything will do as I'm terribly hungry.'

'I've some bread and cheese.'

'That sounds good. Come and join me. What about the others?'

'I've sent theirs out to them. Zak has his with the other two. They cut the grass, you know, and do other odd jobs'

'They don't say much, do they?'

'No, they're a bit simple. They wouldn't do the job if they weren't. They get paid a pittance,' she added bitterly.

'And what about you, Mrs Cooper? Why are you here?'

'I was Mrs Winthrop's maid and came with her when she wed. Gradually, as the servants were dismissed, I had to fit in where I was told.'

'Why did you stay?'

'I couldn't leave Mrs Winthrop, could I? Poor little soul. She was so young and pretty. Now, well…' Her face saddened as she looked back into the past.

Christie said: 'So why do I have to lock my bedroom door, if there are no servants to speak of, to come in.'

Mrs Cooper looked up startled. 'Oh, Miss, I don't know, it's just that Mrs Winthrop thought…'

Christie interrupted. 'That it could be either of the Mr Winthrops?'

'It's not for me to say, Miss,' said Mrs Cooper, looking uncomfortable. Christie said no more.

Apart from Marie Winthrop, Christie saw no one else that day. She went to bed early as she was heartily sick of Marie's company. She had found an old book of poems in one of the rooms and without a by your leave took it upstairs with her. At least it was something to read. Tomorrow she hoped Emma might visit as she had said she would. She certainly couldn't endure any more days like the one she'd just had.

Unfortunately, the next day was more or less a replica of the first. After her breakfast she did manage to see Joel but only briefly. She asked him if he was free to be with her that day so that they could talk but he declined, saying he had work to do. As he was dressed for town she wondered what it could be. Mr Winthrop had said 'Good morning' to her and then shut himself in his study. Marie Winthrop was still having breakfast. She had just finished, however, when Emma called. Christie was hoping to take her sister to her room for a long private chat but Marie had other ideas. They all sat in the withdrawing room and Christie had no real opportunity for a heart to heart with Emma at all. Marie didn't even leave them alone to say goodbye.

Emma returned home with the information that to her Christie seemed bored and unhappy and that she thought Mrs Winthrop was being a 'clinging vine'. Her father said 'what nonsense', and Carrie tried to imagine how Mrs Winthrop 'clung' to Christie.

Christie went to bed early that night so she could be alone and away from the Winthrops. She read some of the poems but they held no pleasure for her. She felt so restless and frustrated that she felt sleep would evade her if she tried to settle down. So she read for a while longer but couldn't concentrate and found herself thinking, 'What am I doing here?' Evidently Joel wasn't interested in her or he would make a bigger push to be more often in her company. Mr Winthrop, she didn't see much of, which, she came to the conclusion, was a good thing. Marie Winthrop had obviously been expected to be with her and entertain her. Two days of her attention, however, had been enough to last a lifetime. Her clothes were dowdy, the house was in need of repair and decorating and obviously there weren't enough servants to do what should be done. The obvious answer, therefore, was that there was a shortage of money. Christie frowned. How could this be? They had cotton fields like the Farrells. But was that why Wilbur Winthrop wanted this alliance so that they could use her money? She thought it was a possibility. Then she remembered what Grandmama had said: "But from what I hear of the Winthrops I wouldn't be too eager to tie the knot, if I were you." So why all this fuss about her marrying Joel? Evidently Papa wanted the marriage for a totally different reason to the Winthrops. A determined little smile came to her lips. That was that, then. She found she had been hoping for an excuse to refuse to marry Joel and now she had. She had tried to like him but who would want to be tied to a husband who didn't really want to know her? He had more or less ignored her since she had been there. Tomorrow, she would declare she was returning home. But she would visit the cotton fields first just to see what they were really like. She would just go and not tell anyone.

She found she felt much happier within herself now she had resolved the situation to her satisfaction. So with a large sigh and a smile as though a great weight had been lifted from her, she placed the book of poems on her bedside table and was just going to blow out the candle when she heard a scraping sound outside her door. The next moment the doorknob turned very slowly.

Chapter 8

Christie held her breath, not daring to move. As the knob turned, the door was pushed. Thank goodness she had remembered to lock it. It was tried again and Christie sat perfectly still. Then a voice whispered, 'Christie'. It was Joel. She relaxed. It was a strong oak door so he couldn't get in unless he battered it down. She smiled to herself. If he couldn't bother to talk to her during the day he certainly wasn't going to be admitted into her bedroom at night. She thought it wouldn't be to talk either and felt embarrassed at the thought.

Then Joel knocked lightly on the door. 'Christie, let me in. I've something for you.'

'I bet you have,' Christie thought and still kept silent. Eventually after nothing happened the door was kicked and muttered words like 'bitch' came to Christie's ears. If she wanted convincing about leaving in the morning this incident convinced her. After Joel had moved away, quite noisily, Christie blew out the candle and with a satisfied smile cuddled down to sleep.

She packed her bags ready to take her leave after breakfast next day. She couldn't just walk out, of course, as she would have liked—that would have been very rude indeed; but she was determined to speak to Mrs Winthrop as soon as she had come downstairs and breakfasted. She would explain that, as Joel couldn't be bothered to even see her, let alone talk to her, she was returning home, now, this minute. She would be very firm about that.

First, though, as she had promised herself, she would see the cotton fields. She expected her father to ask about them, anyway. So she went to find Zak. He was rubbing down the carriage horse in case it was needed.

'Good morning, Zak,' said Christie. 'Could I take the carriage into town, do you think? Then I want to visit the cotton fields. Do you know where they are?'

Zak looked at her out of scared eyes. 'I don't know, Miss.'

'Do you really not know or are you frightened to tell me?' Zak nodded.

'Well, can you point me in the right direction, then you won't have told me, will you?' She smiled. So Zak pointed.

'Have you ever been there?'

He shook his head.

'Do you think I could have the carriage then? I only want to find some food to take with me. I shan't be long, I promise.'

So Zak hurried up to get the horse and carriage ready and they were soon on their way. Christie kept her fingers crossed that they didn't see any of the Winthrops. A supply of fruit and cookies was soon bought, some of which were given to Zak, then Christie asked him to stop at the nearest point so that she could walk to the cotton fields. Zak was told to go back and not say a word.

It was a lovely clear morning, not so warm as of late but as Christie strode along she noticed no chill. She enjoyed a walk and had been deprived of exercise while she had been away from home. For a young, active person she had felt quite confined since she had been at the Winthrops'. It felt good to stride out and as she did so she looked about her with interest. The Winthrops' home was to the far right, so the land in between there and where she was standing was theirs also. Then it curved round, and probably to the slaves' area and the fields beyond. Somewhere, though, it must join with the Farrells' land and the river. She continued her walk and wondered if she should have found out more before she left. She should have asked earlier on, but who would have told her? Certainly not Mrs Winthrop. Joel and his father had kept out of her way and she expected that this morning they might not welcome her. She shrugged; what could they do to her apart from scold? She continued walking. Perhaps Papa knew more about it than what he had told her, or perhaps he didn't think she would want to be bothered about such things. She stopped to draw breath, the goods she was carrying making her puff slightly. She looked about her. Here were the fields—but where were the workers? Then she saw them, a line of women, men and some children. They were silent and slow. Christie noticed that the fields, which should have been prepared ready for winter, were nowhere near that stage. What had the Winthrops been thinking of to let it go so long without attention? She gazed around in surprise. Then the black people began to notice her there. They weren't hostile but just stood still, looking at her as though they hadn't seen a white woman before. Perhaps they hadn't! Christie stepped forward and offered them some fruit. They looked at her blankly. She took one woman's hand, placing an apple in it and said, 'For you.' A glimmer came into the dead eyes. Then Christie went to each one in turn giving a piece of fruit, which they began to eat. A young boy of about twelve gave a small grin.

Christie asked him, 'Where do you live?' There was no response. 'Where are the little boys?' Obviously no one talked to them in English. She pointed to him. 'You are a big boy. Where are the little boys?' She indicated the size with her hand. One of the women, who must have understood some of her words, said something to the boy who pointed.

'Show me,' said Christie, smiling and holding out her hand. After a moment the boy responded and took her hand in his dirty one and led her to an opening. She saw a sight she'd never forget. On the dry and dusty ground makeshift living quarters using branches from trees, broken bricks, dried mud and stones were put together in a haphazard fashion. The shelters were inadequate and gave no protection from the hot sun or rain. Even the trees that were left were poor specimens as many of their branches had been used or burnt on the fire. It looked a derelict area. Little children sat with old people who were trying to cook something on an open fire in a cracked pot. Most of them had the same dead look in their eyes.

When they saw Christie they sat very still, no doubt wondering who she was and what she wanted. The little ones, feeling something was wrong, looked up too, their fingers in their mouths. One began to cry. Christie looked at them in disbelief. They weren't black, although they had the black curly hair, but their skin was a coffee colour. A memory surged up in Christie's mind of the young black girl saying, 'Do white men come?' What white men came here? Joel? Christie stood rooted to the spot. She couldn't really believe it but, on second thoughts, found she could. She moved at last and began to distribute the fruit and cookies with the aid of her little helper who seemed to enjoy himself. A tall, thin man who had been sitting watching, stood with difficulty, then came slowly towards Christie. He looked at her and gave a little nod.

Christie smiled. 'What is your name?' she asked.

He answered her indistinctly, but it sounded like Reuben. So that is what she called him and it brought a smile to his face. By now all the men, women and children had come to see Christie. They stood in small groups and were silent but looked hopeful. 'Reuben, do you all have enough food and water?' She made movements to indicate eating and drinking. Reuben shrugged and shook his head.

Christie nodded. 'I will try and do something about it,' she said, but wondered even as she said it what she could achieve. She wouldn't be able to tackle either of the Winthrops about it; they would resent her interference but she could tell her father, especially when she went home later today and told him how things stood here. She was still thinking and automatically watching as her little helper distributed the food for her when a voice said roughly:

'What in God's name are you doing here? Does old Wilbur know?'

As Christie turned, the black people moved backwards, fear in their eyes. Joel was walking unsteadily towards her, an empty bottle and whip in one hand, the other endeavouring to fasten his breeches. He was drunk.

'I wondered where you were,' Christie said scornfully, eyeing his movements in disgust. She thought she had better take a firm stance and not be intimidated. Out of the corner of her eye there was a movement. She looked and saw a young black girl slip to the nearest cluster of branches. Joel followed Christie's gaze and grinned at her.

'One of the advantages of being the boss!' he shouted.

'You are despicable!' she said. 'Are all these yours?' She pointed to the light-coloured children.

Joel laughed. 'Devil a bit, of course not.'

'Whose, then?' She opened her eyes wide as the truth dawned on her.

'Well, the old man has to have his entertainment sometime, you know.'

'Neither of you are fit to be in charge of these people.'

'People?' said Joel. 'Where?' He came closer, walking unsteadily.

'You keep away from me,' said Christie. 'You are a disgrace.' She stood, hands on hips, facing him.

'You, my girl,' he slurred his words slightly, 'are speaking to your future husband.'

'No I am not,' said Christie, loudly and angrily. 'For goodness' sake get back to the house, if you can walk that far, which I doubt.'

Joel looked ugly. 'Don't tell me what to do, you're only a woman.'

'You are disgusting.'

'And how did you come here anyway? Who showed you the way?' His eyes alighted on the 'little helper'.

'You,' shouted Joel pointing. 'Come here.'

The boy looked scared and stood still. Joel lurched forward and dragged him to stand in front of him. There was a gasp from someone, probably his mother.

Christie moved quickly and placed her hand on the boy's head. 'Leave him alone, Joel, he's only a little boy.'

'He needs a whipping!' shouted Joel, handling his whip suggestively.

'You drunken beast, Joel Winthrop, leave these people alone and go home.'

This fanned Joel's anger even more. 'Don't speak to me like that, you trollop.'

Christie didn't hesitate. She gave him a stinging blow across his cheek with the flat of her hand. 'And don't speak to me like that ever again!' she shouted.

Then Joel raised his whip.

'Go on!' shouted Christie angrily. 'Hit him. Hit a little boy, you coward.'

Then as the whip came down towards the boy, in a flash Christie covered him with her own body, her back towards Joel. And Joel struck! The whirring lash cut her back sharply. There was a gasp from the black people as Christie felt a stinging, searing pain. Then Joel raised his whip a second time and Christie felt it catch the side of her face. The pain was unbelievable. She was robbed of breath, she was shocked, she was falling. Then mercifully it all went black.

Those watching held their breath, horror on their faces. They didn't move. In Joel's befuddled state only a glimmer of the seriousness of his actions penetrated his mind. He flung whip and bottle to the ground and with a flow of colourful curses he lurched off towards the house.

The girls had breakfasted as usual. Emma asked Charlotte and Carrie if they could find time to visit Christie later that morning. She said it would be a good idea if two of them went, as one could talk to Mrs Winthrop while Christie could tell the other in private how everything was progressing. Emma felt really worried about her sister, she told them.

'Charlotte,' said Carrie, once more the organiser, 'I will talk to Mrs Winthrop while you have quiet words with Christie. If you keep a smile on your face all the time Christie is talking to you, no matter what she tells you, Mrs Winthrop won't be worried.'

Charlotte nodded looking at her sister with awe. 'You are very devious, aren't you? But I think it's a good idea. Don't worry Emma, we will find out the truth. You never know, it all might be wonderful.'

Emma sighed. 'I do hope so, but somehow I doubt it.'

Eventually they were ready to go, Jacob and the carriage waiting. They decided not to say goodbye to their father and disturb him as he was in his study with Mr Pope the accountant. So bonnets on, light shawls round their shoulders, they trod down the steps of the Hall. As they started to climb into the carriage they saw a figure striding across the grass towards the house. It was Joseph. He was struggling slightly as in his arms he carried a figure. It was Christie. Charlotte was the first to move. 'Good gracious, Carrie, fetch Papa—quickly!' She picked up her skirts, jumped down on to the path and ran to meet Joseph.

'What is it? What has happened?' she called breathlessly.

'Miss Christie is in very bad way,' panted Joseph.

Charlotte looked in horror. Christie was still unconscious and blood was on her dress, hair and face. As Charlotte couldn't do anything to help her, she ran back to the waiting Jacob. 'Go and find the doctor and bring him back, please, Jacob. Tell him it's Miss Christie and it's urgent!'

Jacob cast one worried look at the approaching Joseph, told the horse to start then clattered off at a great rate.

Then Thomas came on the scene. He looked stunned when he saw Christie in Joseph's arms. 'What happened?' he asked as he took Christie from him.

Joseph shrugged. 'Don't know, Mr Farrell, black people not do it.'

'Who did then?'

'Miss Christie will say,' said Joseph and he turned quickly away. As Thomas carried his daughter to her bedchamber, Charlotte thanked Joseph and told him to go and see Zilpah for refreshment. Also to tell her what had occurred. As Thomas laid Christie on her bed he stared in horror at her bloodied face and torn dress. Then Emma came in looking pale and trembling.

'How has she come to be like this? What shall we do?' asked Emma, wringing her hands.

But she had no time to help in any way as Zilpah bustled through the doorway.

'All right,' she said, taking charge. She had brought with her a bowl of water and clean cloths. 'I see to everyt'ing for when doctor come.'

Thomas sat down. 'Why doesn't she wake up? I want to know what happened.'

'She wake when she's ready,' said Zilpah, 'but I want to make her comfortable as I can before she does. Now as I have to undress her, you had better wait downstairs, Mis' Farrell, and take dose girls with you.' She indicated Charlotte and Carrie who were hovering.

'Yes, yes, of course. Thank you, Zilpah.' He left looking confused but with a mixture of anger and disbelief at what he had seen. Emma came in to find that Zilpah had undone Christie's dress as far as she could. The frayed edges of the cotton stuck to the bloodied gash down her back. Gently she bathed the wound, pulling away the back of the dress. When the whole was removed, she cleaned the wound on her face and where the whip had caught her neck. Although the wounds were deep, they were clean now. Emma felt faint; she had never seen so much blood.

'What can we use to heal the cuts?' asked Emma, paler than ever.

'We wait for de doctor man,' said Zilpah. 'He tell us. I wonder who did dis to her?'

'Do you think someone did it on purpose or was it an accident?'

Zilpah shrugged. 'I dunno but it look like whip to me. I seen plenty of dose,' she nodded.

Emma placed her hand on Zilpah's arm fleetingly. 'Do you think it was the slaves? And how did Joseph find her?'

'I dunno,' Zilpah said again, 'but Miss Christie will tell us later.' She looked at Emma's pale face. 'Why don't you go and wait for de doctor man, Miss Emma. I stay here.'

Emma nodded with relief as she felt rather queasy but still anxious about her sister.

'We find out when she tell us. You go now, Miss Emma. I'll stay wit' your sister til doctor man come.'

Zilpah sat by the bed after Emma had left, watching Christie. She shook her head at the troubles a scarred face would arouse in the future and wept deep down inside her for her young mistress.

Before long the doctor arrived. He had known the Farrells a long time and had been a friend for many years. Thomas told him briefly all that he knew and then Emma accompanied the doctor upstairs. He was pleased with Zilpah's administrations, took Christie's pulse and felt her head. He nodded and then began to make pads for the wounds smeared with healing herbal creams. He told Zilpah to fetch plenty of fruit juice for Christie to drink as she would be very thirsty as shock set in. He and Emma stayed while this was done and Christie began to stir. As she opened her eyes, Emma rushed to her side. 'It's all right, dear,' she said. 'You are home and safe.'

The doctor nodded but held up his hand to halt more words. Then as Christie moved she felt the pain and the bandaging. When Zilpah came back she poured out a glass of the juice and handed it to Christie who managed to sit up a little with the sheet pulled around her. She drank it and tried to speak.

'I want to see Papa.' Her voice was husky and breathless.

'I will fetch him, dear,' Emma said and rushed from the room.

Thomas came immediately. 'Thank goodness you are better, my love. Whatever happened?' He went quickly towards Christie to place his arms around her but the doctor stopped him.

'She is ill, Mr Farrell. Sit by the bed and just listen, please.'

Thomas stopped abruptly but did as he was told, looking rather perplexed.

'Papa,' whispered Christie.

Startled, Thomas looked at the doctor. 'Her voice,' he said, 'what's the matter?'

'It's all right. It's the shock. It will right itself. Just listen, she can't talk for long.' So Thomas contained himself and listened.

'Papa. Please help the Winthrops' workers. They need food and shelter. Go and see and take Joseph with you. Promise?'

'Yes of course, but why Joseph?'

'He speaks their language. Do help them, Papa, please.' By now she was exhausted and curled up on her side trying to get comfortable.

'But Christie, who did this to you?'

She had her eyes closed but managed to whisper 'Joel.' Tears seeped from beneath her eyelids.

Thomas wanted to ask further questions but the doctor would not allow it. 'Come along, old fellow, leave her to rest. She'll be able to tell you more in a day or two. I shall give her a cordial which will help her.'

After this was administered, Christie was left in peace to blissful sleep with Zilpah keeping watch beside her.

Chapter 9

Thomas sat in his study, his head in his hands. What had really happened? Of course he believed Christie when she said Joel had used his whip on her, but *why* had he done so? Surely he couldn't have done it on purpose? It must have been an accident. He hoped so, but it did not make it any better for his daughter. She would have scars forever. He should not have let her go to stay; it was his fault but he thought she had wanted to go. Then after Emma had visited and said Christie wasn't happy, he had not listened to her, saying that it was nonsense. So what was to be done? He had better go and visit the Winthrops and see what it was all about. Also, he must visit their workers. He could not really interfere here, but he had promised Christie and she would want to know the result. She had also told him to take Joseph. Well, he would do that too, but he did not think Wilbur would like it.

So he put on his coat, sent for Jacob and the carriage and informed Emma where he was going. Then they went to find Joseph to accompany him, to see the Winthrops' workers. Joseph just nodded and sat with Jacob.

They arrived at the Winthrops' home and Thomas told them to stay in the carriage, while he trod up the steps and rang the bell. Nothing happened. He rang again. After a wait of perhaps five minutes, the door was opened by Wilbur himself, who looked very much displeased. His attitude changed, though, when he saw who it was. Thomas was surprised at him answering his own doorbell and said so. Wilbur passed it off with a laugh and said jovially: 'The servants didn't hear, I suppose. But come in, come in, you will want to see your daughter, I expect.'

'No,' said Thomas, keeping his temper in check. 'It's you I've come to see, and Joel.'

'Come in the study. I'm afraid Joel is down in the fields working.'

'Really?'

'Sit down. Cigar?'

'No, thank you. How is your wife? Well, I hope?' Thomas was trying hard to keep his temper.

'Yes, she was so pleased to have Christie for company, you know. They've been out shopping and having a lovely time by all accounts. But I haven't seen them today, I'm so busy, you know.' He laughed again. 'We men always have our, er—shoulders to the wheel, don't we?'

'Wilbur, I'm not going to beat...' Thomas once more had to rein his temper as a knock sounded on the door. It opened and Marie Winthrop came in.

'Oh, there you are, my dear. Here is Thomas. I was just telling him how pleased we are to have Christie.'

'Oh, I'm sorry, I didn't know.' Mrs Winthrop looked paler than usual. She clutched at her dress. 'That's what I came about, Wilbur. I'm sorry, so sorry but I can't find her anywhere. I went to her room and I found she had packed her things. She didn't tell me she was going. But I can't find her! Have you seen her?' She was wringing her hands by now.

Her husband glared at her but before he could say anything Thomas, not holding back any longer, shouted: 'She is at home, Mrs Winthrop! Joseph brought her.' Now he raised his voice even more. 'She was unconscious and bleeding! She told me later that Joel had used his whip on her!'

'No, no,' murmured Marie breathlessly and would have fallen if Thomas had not had the presence of mind to catch her and place her in his vacated chair.

Wilbur was on his feet, his face suffused with red. 'No, no she must be wrong! He wouldn't do that when they are to wed. It's not too bad though, is it?' he asked hopefully.

'Yes it is! She is wounded on her face, neck and back, and I've had the doctor to her. He's given her a draught to make her sleep. So I want to know what the hell has been going on here and why you've not been looking after my daughter and let your damned son treat her in such a way? Where is he?'

'Er, he'll be working, I expect. I'll send for him, it's easier than going all that way. You just sit there while I sort things out.' He was still jovial but Thomas could tell he was angry and this was not something he was happy about. He was obviously trying to prevent Thomas from going to the fields, so perversely Thomas was determined to go. This is why Christie went, perhaps? She knew something was not right.

So Thomas said: 'It's no trouble, my carriage is outside, we can go in that. What about your wife? She needs help.'

'Oh, I'll call Mrs Cooper as we go out,' he answered offhandedly, and without another thought for his wife, marched through the door yelling for Mrs Cooper, followed by Thomas. As they left Mrs Cooper came running.

Wilbur said no more and the journey was quiet, but Thomas noticed that although Wilbur had given no instructions to Jacob how to get to the fields that was definitely where they were going. How did he know the way? Or how did Joseph? They arrived. 'You stay there, I'll find Joel,' said Wilbur, the last bright idea he could think of to stop Thomas going with him.

'No, no,' said Thomas determinedly. 'Christie said I was to go and take Joseph. You come with me, Joseph. Jacob, you stay here.' Somehow, he didn't know why, but Thomas felt more comfortable to have the large black man with him but Wilbur frowned, not pleased at all.

They walked over to the clearing where the slaves lived. Thomas, like Christie, was shocked at the conditions. The workers who were there and not in the fields looked at Thomas with anxious eyes. Thomas noticed how frightened and thin they were. Wilbur seemed not to notice.

'Where is Mr Winthrop?' he shouted. He grabbed hold of one of the women. 'Where's my son?'

She didn't answer but looked extremely frightened. Thomas stepped in and pulled Wilbur's hand away. 'Leave her! Who is the head one?'

'I don't know, they're all the same.'

'No,' said Thomas. He turned to Joseph. 'Do you know who is in charge? We would like to speak to him.'

Joseph said something in their language and Reuben stepped forward. 'This is Reuben,' Joseph said to Thomas. He shook Reuben's hand.

'Do you know where Mr Joel Winthrop is?'

Reuben nodded and pointed to the house. In his own language he said 'Gone to his home.' Joseph translated.

'Nonsense,' said Wilbur. 'He must be in the fields.' So they went to the fields.

'Good gracious, man,' said Thomas, aghast when he saw them. 'You are behind here.'

'Well, don't blame me,' said a now surly Wilbur. 'It's Joel's responsibility.'

'You own the place—how has it become like this?' Thomas began to feel that he was in a nightmare. Poor Christie, how she must have felt the same. He wanted to know what had happened and hoped to question the black people. But they would be too frightened to tell him in case of repercussions from Wilbur. It was evident they were a terrified people and by the look of the little ones the Winthrop men had not treated the women kindly either. He could not blame himself enough to think that Christie had seen all this. She must have been horrified.

'We'd better go back to the house and see if he's there, I suppose,' said Wilbur, now in a worse temper than ever and marched off.

Thomas turned to Joseph. 'Ask Reuben what happened, then let me know. Be quick.' Then he followed Wilbur slowly so that Joseph had time to glean the information. A few minutes later Joseph reported as well as he could that Miss Christie had been kind to them. Then Joel had appeared in a drunken state and decided to whip a little boy but Miss Christie had protected him with her body. Thomas nodded. That would be just like her to do a thing like that. On the way back to the house, Thomas sat stony faced, thinking hard. Wilbur felt angry and uncomfortable but dared not say anything.

They entered the house once more, Wilbur bellowing Joel's name. There was no response. Thomas stood in the hall waiting. How wrong he had been to expect Christie to marry into this family. It was his fault that she had been attacked. If he hadn't been so keen for her to marry Joel this would never have happened. He felt very much to blame but the deed had been done so now someone had to pay for it, and that would be the Winthrops. He owed it to Christie. Meanwhile, Wilbur opened all doors calling Joel's name. Then he went upstairs shouting at the top of his voice. Ten minutes later he came down again, slowly. Gone was the bombastic personality. His worst fears having been realised, he was stunned.

He looked at Thomas. 'He's on his bed. Drunk.' He shook his head and went into his study.

Thomas followed. 'Well,' he said when they were seated, 'we have some straight talking to do, you and I, haven't we? From what I've seen of this house no money has been spent on it for years. There are no servants and there has been no money spent on the slaves or the fields. For goodness' sake, man, what have you been doing?'

Wilbur put his face in his hands. The deep red that had suffused it a few minutes ago had now turned to grey. Thomas hoped he would not have to send for the doctor and then wondered why he should bother anyway. As Wilbur said nothing, Thomas went on: 'From what I've seen and I'm sure you will tell me if

I'm wrong, you have wasted all the money you had. Was it gambling and women, Wilbur? Were you and Joel, both of you guilty, I wonder?'

For answer a groan came from the bowed head.

'I assume by that, that I'm right. Also by the results, I again assume that both of you have abused the black women.' As no answer came Thomas shouted, 'Answer me, yes or no!'

Wilbur nodded and whispered 'yes'.

'You are disgusting. How your poor wife must have suffered!'

'What shall I do?' asked Wilbur pathetically.

Thomas walked to the window. He wasn't a violent man but he could quite happily have punched Wilbur on the nose for all the suffering he and Joel had inflicted on the workers throughout the years, and on his darling Christie. Trying to keep his temper in check he looked out the window, thinking hard. After a while he returned and sat down. 'I expect you hoped the money that came with Christie on her marriage to Joel would help solve your problems. It wouldn't have, you know. You and Joel are too greedy. It would have seeped through your fingers in no time. Thank God we found out in time and I wish I hadn't thought of it in the first place. However, I'll tell you what I'll do. And you had better be in agreement with me otherwise I'll have that son of yours up before the authorities for the attempted murder of my daughter.' Thomas was now determined that what he said would be done. It was the least he could do for his daughter.

'What do you propose?'

'To save Christie any embarrassment in the future I will buy Joel a one-way ticket to Europe. You can say he has gone on the Grand Tour. While he is over there he will have to find money somehow to live and the fare for his return journey if he wants to return. The experience, hopefully, might do him some good, but I doubt it. But he will be out of our sight and I shall see him on to the ship myself to check that he has really gone. That's number one. Next, I will see that the cotton fields are returned to what they should be so that the cotton crop is good again in the future.'

Wilbur began to look hopeful. Thomas ignored him and went on: 'Number three. I will provide shelter, food and water and a decent living area for the workers so that they are happy and therefore work better and I will also keep an eye on things. Which means you don't go anywhere near that area. Do I make myself clear?' Thomas drummed his fingers on the desk to emphasise each word and stared into the eyes of the man opposite.

'My dear fellow, that is very generous of you…' began Wilbur, beaming.

Thomas looked at him with distaste. 'I haven't finished. And you, you will go about selling the whole of your property.'

'But—but where will I go? I can't...'

'To be honest with you, you and your son revolt me and I don't want you living next to us or anywhere near us.'

'But—but—' stuttered Wilbur, 'I can run it again if I get help.'

'You've had your chance and I want the money back which I shall be laying out. So you will have to sell your house to repay me. That is all I have to say. Where you and your precious family go I couldn't care less, as long as it is far away from me and my family. I'll get Pope to prepare the agreement which you had better sign or I'll have you in jail.' With that he strode to the door and his waiting carriage. One look at his face and Joseph or Jacob dared not say a thing. However, when they arrived at the Hall, Thomas said to Joseph: 'You've told me how my daughter came by her wounds, but how and where did you find her?'

Joseph said after a minute: 'There is a way from their fields to ours. Reuben carried Miss Christie a little way and the boy ran ahead to fetch me. Then I carried Miss Christie home.'

'I see. How long have you had contact with these other people?'

'Some time. They were desperate for food at times. We let them have some of ours. I'm sorry if I did wrong, but...'

Thomas shook his head. 'No, no, but I wish you had told me.'

'I'm sorry.'

Thomas smiled. 'Thank you, Joseph, and thank you for bringing my daughter home safely.'

'She will be better soon?'

'I hope so, Joseph. I hope so.'

Over the next few weeks Christie's wounds healed well, so much so that the doctor said only a light dressing on her back was needed and none at all on her face and neck. The flesh had knitted well and he was pleased with the result. He told her that now she could return to normal and do the things she usually did. He would not call again, unless, of course, he was needed.

Christie had thanked him but when she looked at herself in the mirror she dissolved into tears. The mark stretching from her right cheekbone to nearly her chin was bright red and still looked sore. Zilpah comforted her as best she could, saying it was early days and the mark would gradually fade. It needed air to heal and she must walk outside. But Christie at eighteen was very conscious of her looks. She said she would stay where she was. Zilpah argued with her as much as she dared but when Christie was so near to tears she had not the heart to press her. Instead, lots of comforting hugs were administered.

Christie saw her father once and he reported on his talk with Wilbur. She thanked him, then said she was tired so he left. She would not see her sisters, only Zilpah, and as the weeks went by they all became used to 'no Christie' around the house. Zilpah, in her role of nurse, had to delegate the cooking to others. It was all working very well but Christie was not improving in her mind. Her scars became less vivid but to her own eyes she looked a mess. She grew thinner from lack of food and exercise. Zilpah was beside herself with worry.

One morning she tried once more. 'Miss Christie, you will get out of dis room today or you will die. Is dat what you want? What has your family done dat you don't want to see dem, huh?'

'Oh Zilpah, nothing. But how can I face anyone looking like this?'

'De scar is improving.'

'Even if the colour goes the skin will still be puckered,' said Christie, her lips trembling.

'People have worse things dan dat on der faces. Why don't you come downstairs. You will feel better. I'm not asking you to walk down the middle of Charleston, am I?'

Christie smiled a little. 'Perhaps another day, Zilpah.'

Shaking her head, Zilpah went to find Mr Farrell but he was out. She went to the girls' room but only Emma was there.

'They all went out but me,' Emma smiled, looking up from her sewing. 'What is it, Zilpah?'

'Miss Christie must leave her room, but she won't. Will you let me go and fetch de Gran'ma Lady, please Miss Emma? She is de only one Miss Christie will listen to. And if she doesn't leave her room soon she will die I'm sure.'

Emma swallowed. 'Yes, well, would it be better if I go, Zilpah, only…'

Zilpah said: 'I can go, Miss Emma. I can look after Gran'ma Lady very good. You stay in case Miss Christie want anyt'ing.'

Emma nodded. She didn't really want to go. Grandmama was an alarming little lady and Emma was always a tiny bit frightened of her.

So soon after, Zilpah and her son Jacob, took the carriage to Grandmama Farrell's house. Zilpah was a little daunted when she saw it and what she proposed doing but told herself it was for Miss Christie's sake. She rang the bell.

The door was opened to her and she asked to see the Gran'ma Lady about Miss Christie. The servant went to find Matty. She spoke to Zilpah and told her to wait and she would see if Mrs Farrell would see her. Evidently she would and

Zilpah climbed the stairs and was shown into her room. Mrs Farrell was taking tea and looked up when Zilpah entered. Matty hovered at the door, not knowing whether to stay or go. She was told to go and bring another teacup. Matty opened her eyes wide, but encountering a piercing stare, hurried away.

'Well?'

Zilpah swallowed. 'I'm Zilpah and I look after Miss Christie de last few weeks but she won't leave her bedchamber. Could you come, please, and—and make her? She unhappy.' Zilpah felt uncomfortable. This little lady was frightening.

'Sit down.'

Zilpah sat. Matty came back with a teacup. Mrs Farrell poured tea into it and indicated that Matty should give it to Zilpah. Zilpah was overawed. A great lady had offered her tea! If it were possible, Gran'ma Lady had climbed further in her estimation.

'Well, why won't my granddaughter come out of her bedchamber?'

'You not hear about her visit to the Wint'rops, ma'am?'

'Ah. No, tell me.'

'Miss Christie went to stay. She brought home a few days later, unconscious and bloody. She been beaten wit' a whip. Mr Farrell sent for de doctor. Miss Christie is better now but won't come out of her room 'cos of de scar. I done my best but…'

Mrs Farrell interrupted. 'Has her father tried?'

'Ye-es but she won't see anyone but me. It not right, Gran'ma Lady, but I don't know what else to do?'

Mrs Farrell stared at Zilpah, a little smile playing round her mouth. Eventually she said: 'You did right to come, Zilpah. Please ring the bell.'

Matty appeared. 'I'm visiting Farrell Hall. Now.'

Matty gasped. '*Now*, Ma'am?'

'Yes, now, you stupid creature. Help me downstairs and find my cloak. Did your son bring the carriage?'

Zilpah opened her eyes wide. 'Yes, oh yes. He's waiting.'

'Jacob, isn't it?'

'Yes, Gran'ma Lady.'

'Did you know he likes one of my young servant girls?'

'Yes, but if you don't like…'

'You can tell him I don't object as long as he treats her properly. She's a nice little lass.'

'T'ank you, I tell him,' said Zilpah, showing her white teeth in a lovely smile. The day was becoming better and better. If only the Gran'ma Lady could do something about Miss Christie, Zilpah thought this would be a day to remember.

Chapter 10

Thomas had just arrived home and was mounting the steps, when he heard the carriage brought to a standstill on the gravel behind him. He frowned when he saw Jacob and even more when he saw Zilpah climb down.

'What is going on here?' he shouted, descending the steps once more. When he saw his mother, however, he stopped dead in his tracks. 'Mother?'

Zilpah had by this time tenderly helped the old lady down. Mrs Farrell, her arm in Zilpah's, began to climb the steps slowly, saying as she did so: 'If you stopped bellowing, Thomas, and came to help me, it would be of more use.'

Thomas immediately went to the other side of her. 'But what are you doing here, Mama? Why?'

'We'll discuss things inside.'

He led her into the morning room and she told Zilpah to wait in the hall and then sat down.

'I'm here because Zilpah asked me to come. Evidently she thinks I can help Christie which you, her father, cannot.' She glared at him.

'I've tried, Mother, I really have.'

'Why didn't you send for me earlier then?'

'Well, I didn't think. I just hoped she would be all right when the wounds healed.'

'Mmm. Just like a man! You're a fool. Always were,' she finished with a sniff.

Thomas said nothing. His mother had always been sharp tongued. It was no good arguing with her and now she was old he didn't want to upset her and make her ill. If he knew her, though, she probably guessed that this is what he thought and so felt she could be as obnoxious as she liked. She would find it enjoyable.

Mrs Farrell looked at her son and guessed what he was thinking. Her face softened. 'All right, Thomas, arguing won't get us anywhere.' A little smile played round her lips. 'Do you know what Zilpah calls me?'

'No,' said Thomas, wondering what was coming next.

'She calls me 'Gran'ma Lady', isn't that charming?'

Thomas only had time to smile before there was a knock on the door and Emma looked in. 'May I come in a moment? Thank you for coming, Grandmama. Zilpah asked me, Papa, if she could go and ask Grandmama to come. She knows Christie will listen to her. You weren't home.'

'I see, that...'

Mrs Farrell broke in: 'That was sensible of you, Emma. I will chat to you later and the other girls if they are home. But let us see what we can do about Christie. Send Zilpah to me and you two go away.' She waved in the direction of the door.

After a minute Zilpah came in. 'Yes, Gran'ma Lady?'

'Go to Miss Christie and tell her I am here to see her. Tell her it will take me a long time to climb all those stairs but that is what I shall do if she won't come down.' She nodded and Zilpah left.

Ten minutes later the door opened and Christie stood there. Her Grandmama opened her arms and said simply, 'Come here, my love.'

Christie ran to her, dropping on to her knees and burying her face in her Grandmama's lap. Mrs Farrell ran her gnarled fingers gently over her hair, saying soothingly, 'It's all right, Christie, really it is. I've come especially to see you, dear.'

Eventually Christie looked up slowly. Her Grandmama took out a lavender scented handkerchief and mopped Christie's face. 'Here, you take it, you'll make a better job of it. Now tell me why you are so loath to leave your bedchamber.'

So Christie told her in a jumbled way what had happened. Mrs Farrell listened patiently, then said: 'Christie, you have to put all this behind you now, and get on with life. You are young after all. Will you show me the scars?'

Christie held up her face. Grandmama pushed back her hair. Poor girl, she could understand how she felt, but she smiled. 'Well, now. It will go away eventually. In the meantime, can you brush your hair to this side and have it over your shoulder? It will hide most of it, you know. Then as the air gets to it, it will heal.' Christie nodded, sniffing tearfully.

'So, looking back, Christie, are you sorry you protected the little boy?'

Christie looked up quickly. 'Oh no, poor little mite. I would do it again. The only thing was, you see, I didn't expect Joel would use his whip on me.'

'Well, there you are. You would do it again but we know now that Joel is violent and uncontrolled and a libertine amongst other things. So forget him and move on. When we talked before you said you would like to travel. How about it? Where would you like to go? A long way away?'

'Ye-es, it could be a good idea, but where and when? I don't know.'

'Don't sound so negative. Let me have a word with your Father. I have an idea. Meanwhile, go and talk to your sisters, if you remember what they look like. I'll see them before I go.'

So Christie left to find Emma and Thomas rejoined his mother.

'I suggest,' she said without preamble, 'that Christie goes away for a while to regain her confidence. It will do her good mentally and physically. And a change of scenery will be beneficial, I think.'

'But where?'

'I think it would be sensible to have someone to look after her for a while. What about Cousin Amelia?'

'But she lives in England.'

'I know she lives in England, that's why I'm suggesting it. It will be different and do her the world of good. She will be interested to see where we originated. Write and ask if Christie can stay with her.'

'But it will be wintertime.'

'Really, Thomas, you are most tiresome with your buts. Of course it will be wintertime. That's when everything livens up after the summer. She'll enjoy it all and it will be different. Amelia was always kind and fun to be with.'

'Very well, I'll ask Christie and then I'll write.'

'Good. By the time you have a reply Christie should be much improved.'

In the weeks that followed Christie did improve. Her sisters were a great help and support to her. They sympathised and were gentle at the beginning but as she grew stronger, they began to treat her as their big sister once more. She began to eat properly and as she immersed herself in the running of the household once again she became nearly her usual self. But not quite, she had received a severe blow in more ways than one. However, she looked much better and Carrie helped her to arrange her hair as Grandmama had suggested so that only a little of the scar near her chin showed. Charlotte reported upon the progress of the black people and told her they always asked after her and were concerned.

Thomas eventually had a reply to his letter from Cousin Amelia in England saying she would be delighted for Christie to visit and expected to see her sometime in December. All would be made ready for her and she would have someone check the ships' arrivals so that a carriage would be waiting for her.

Christie, feeling better, wondered if she needed to go away now. She felt apprehensive about travelling over the sea to an unknown new life, even if it were only for a short time in England. Papa had told her that Joel had already set sail for Europe so she would not see him around any more. She talked to Grandmama again and she began to feel that perhaps it was a good thing to go away. It would at least be interesting and something completely different. Grandmama had evidently talked to Zilpah who had agreed to accompany Christie. For this she was grateful, as she knew Zilpah would be a good companion too. When asked if she would mind leaving Jacob, she had said he was old enough to look after himself, and also that the 'Gran'ma Lady' had hoped she would go with Christie to look after her. So that is what she, Zilpah, would do.

So the next thing was to choose warm clothing to take and the girls had fun helping Christie shop. Thomas said he would make arrangements for her to draw money from a bank in Bristol, which was the largest town near to Stanton where Cousin Amelia Ford lived. Zilpah also had warm clothes bought and by the beginning of November all was ready, Thomas having booked their passage.

The day before Christie left, Charlotte asked her to go once more to see Joseph and the others. So she accompanied Charlotte and her father to say goodbye. When they arrived Christie couldn't believe her eyes as there were more people than she had seen before. Then she noticed the light coloured children and knew that the workers from the Winthrops' plantation had walked all the way just to see her and wish her well. Joseph explained that they wanted to thank her for what she had done for them. The little boy, whom she had saved from a whipping, handed her a red flower. Then the adults began to sing. It was a song about being happy, Joseph explained. Christie, Charlotte and Thomas stood and listened to the beautiful harmonies that came so naturally to the black people's singing. When it finished Christie had tears running down her cheeks, she was so moved. She clapped them all and smiled, then moved among them to thank them before returning home.

Next day Thomas saw Christie and Zilpah off as they boarded the ship, which was to take them to England.

Chapter 11

▼

Only Thomas had seen Christie and Zilpah board the *Sea Swallow*, the sailing ship that was to take them far away to England. Christie had said her farewells to her sisters at home and apart from waving to Papa from the deck of the ship when they first boarded, she and Zilpah had gone straightaway to their cabins. Long goodbyes were not to Thomas's taste.

Now Christie sat on her 'bed', a wooden area packed with blankets, which she inspected and sniffed to make sure they weren't stale. She looked round at the small area that was to be her home for the next few weeks. The facilities were adequate and it was clean. She heard the running feet of the sailors on deck and the orders for the anchor to be raised. After more shouting and noise the sails were unfurled and the *Sea Swallow* began to move. The long journey across the Atlantic had begun.

Christie told herself everything would be fine and that she would be a good sailor. She hoped Zilpah would be, too. As the ship surged forward, the wind in her sails, she felt a weird feeling of helplessness. Still, she thought, while she was experiencing the different sensations and sounds, she had not time to think of Papa and the girls. She missed them already after the tearful goodbyes. It would be some time before she saw them again. Would they have altered so much, she wondered? But she would not think of them, not yet, anyway, only when she knew she was strong enough not to shed tears. So she resolutely thought of things to come. Would Cousin Amelia be fun to be with as Grandmama had said? And would she like Christie to call her Cousin? After all, she was Papa's cousin, not hers; and would Stanton, where she lived near Bristol, be a pretty place? Would

Bristol be larger than Charleston? What a lot of new things to see and learn about! She only hoped the people would be friendly.

Zilpah had a cabin next to Christie's for which they were both pleased and now Christie went to make sure she was settled in. She gave a tap on the door and opened it. 'Is everything all right, Zilpah?' she asked.

'Yes, Miss Christie, but how we manage in such tiny space for so long, I just don't know.' She shook her head.

'I expect we shall get used to it,' said Christie hopefully.

She was invited that evening, together with three other couples, to dine at the Captain's table. They were the only passengers apart from the servants, who dined elsewhere. Zilpah was pleased to find another black lady among these to talk to who was a maid to one of the ladies. Christie felt a little on her own when dining but as the Captain was on his own it made an even number. He was an older man who had been at sea for some years, as his weather-beaten face proclaimed. The food was plain and a little greasy but otherwise good. The wine was somewhat heavy, so Christie took very little. She learnt that the others were sailing to London, then on to the Continent, so they had a longer journey than she had. She did not envy them.

A routine emerged for Christie. She and Zilpah would walk on the deck in the morning, weather permitting. Then Christie would meet one of the couples for a chat while Zilpah cleaned their rooms and made, as she said, 'everyt'ing right'. Then they would rest or in Christie's case, read. There would be more walking or sitting on deck depending on the weather, in the afternoon, then after the evening meal another walk on the deck before retiring. Christie noticed people sometimes looking at her and knew they wondered about the scar although they did not say a word to her. She did try to cover it, but on deck, when the breeze blew her hair it was sometimes difficult to do so. She did wear her cloak and hood as the days became colder, which helped. They experienced one or two squalls and storms. Then they kept to their cabins, their stomachs not able to cope with the tossing and the turbulence.

Christie had brought two books with her. One was a novel, called *Faraway Land,* that Charlotte had given to her and which, of course, she had already read. Christie had now read this twice. She also had a little book of poems, which she had read once. Now to pass the time Christie read to Zilpah to amuse them both. She suspected, though, that Zilpah was not really interested but she listened because it gave them something to do. And so the days passed by.

It was after they had been at sea nearly two months and the end of the year was approaching that the news went round one day that land was in sight. So by the following morning, Christie and Zilpah were ready to disembark. They said their goodbyes and thanked the Captain and wished everyone a safe voyage to London and the Continent.

Christie heaved a large sigh as she was so glad to leave the ship behind her; she was heartily sick of the limited space they had had. She had eaten very little during the latter part of the voyage. What she thought was good food at the beginning palled after a while, as there was little variety. So she had lost weight, much to Zilpah's concern. She, though, seemed to be her usual cuddly self. She remonstrated with Christie. 'You all skin and bone, Miss Christie. What will your Cousin Amelia say? She say, "Zilpah, you not look after Miss Christie properly." Dat's what she'll say.'

She and Zilpah negotiated the gangway to stand once more on the firm ground of the quayside. They still felt the rolling gait of the *Sea Swallow* as they stood there waiting for their trunks and baggage to be brought and Christie was pleased to be able to hold on to Zilpah.

'So this is Bristol,' she said. 'And we are now in England.' She tried to convince herself that they had really arrived.

On the quay was all hustle and bustle. Seamen, with their bags of possessions, shouted to each other, pleased to be home. Some fought to be first into the liquor houses and brothels not far away. Empty barrels were being rolled off the ships and filled ones rolled on. All was mayhem.

Christie and Zilpah, their baggage now at their feet, looked round wondering what they should do. They hugged themselves inside their cloaks as the icy wind blew. Christie wondered if she should try and find a carriage to take them to Stanton but she really did not know where to look. So they continued to wait hoping that Cousin Amelia was as good as her word and had checked the *Sea Swallow*'s arrival date. They still waited and Christie began to feel that she should do something soon as they were being stared at now and she felt uncomfortable. Apart from that, it was decidedly cold, the wind whipping round the corner of the buildings. At that moment, a tall gentleman dressed all in black came hurrying along. He had a lined face, a grey wig and a black hat, which he had difficulty holding on to.

'Miss Farrell?' he called, doffing the same black hat and holding on to his wig with his other hand, his voice fluctuating as the wind took it. 'I am Francis Wicks. I have come to meet you. I am so sorry you have been kept waiting.'

He shook hands with Christie, always keeping one hand on his head. His thin lips smiled. 'I have a carriage waiting. Please follow me.' He snapped his fingers at some idlers and told them to bring the baggage.

They did not have to walk too far to where the carriage stood. The driver opened the door and let down the steps, which they both thankfully climbed, and sat down inside on the well-upholstered seat. Trunks and baggage were soon stowed away and it was not long before Mr Wicks joined them and they were off. He asked solicitously about their journey and if they were well, before saying: 'I am Mrs Ford's lawyer and I am sorry I have to impart some sad news.'

'Oh dear,' said Christie, her heart missing a beat. 'Is Mrs Ford ill?'

'Well, I am afraid since she wrote the letter to your Father, she had a fall in the icy weather and caught a chill. This affected her lungs and I'm sorry to say she died two weeks ago. I am so sorry,' he repeated as he heard Christie gasp. He went on: 'I have taken charge of things, of course, and at the moment all is ready for you and you will stay in the house for the time being. That is all you need to know at the present. I can tell you in a day or two how things stand. Do not worry,' he added, seeing the look of disappointment on Christie's face, 'The housekeeper is very helpful and all will be well.' He smiled.

'Thank you for meeting us and explaining it all, Mr Wicks. When was the funeral?'

'Three days ago. The staff, of course, are very upset and wonder what will happen. But we will discuss it all later when you have settled in. They realise that you would expect to see Mrs Ford.'

'Yes, indeed. I was so looking forward to meeting her.'

For the rest of the journey Christie wondered what would happen now with no Cousin Amelia. She could have wept as she had hoped to find someone new to confide in and to take care of her for a while. However, Mr Wicks said he had everything under control and no doubt he would tell her more in due course. But all she wanted to do at the moment was to have something good to eat and a long sleep in a comfortable bed.

Chapter 12

Amelia Ford's house lay on the northern or Bristol side of Stanton, so that the carriage soon came to an abrupt halt outside the door without having to travel the length of the village. It was an unprepossessing house with slender Doric columns either side the doorway and windows that overlooked the street. By Christie's standards it was quite small but she was cheered slightly by the mellow look of the stone and the quietness of the area. The crape bow tied on the doorknocker, though, was a sad reminder of Mrs Ford's demise.

As they stepped down from the carriage, the oak door opened to reveal a middle-aged woman dressed in black. She curtseyed slightly as they advanced and Mr Wicks introduced them. 'This is Mrs Cardew who will look after you for the time being.'

Christie held out her hand. 'Thank you, Mrs Cardew. It must be a trying time for you just now. I am sorry we have to add to your trouble.'

Mrs Cardew smiled. 'It is unfortunate but we will do what we can to make you comfortable, ma'am,' she said.

Then, as she eyed Zilpah doubtfully, Christie said: 'This is Zilpah. She helps with everything.' Zilpah gave a little bob like she was used to at Farrell Hall and smiled her lovely, dazzling smile.

Inside the servants stood in a line to be introduced. Mary, Mrs Ford's dresser, Mrs Parsloe the cook, Bella the maid who evidently looked after most things, and a little maid of all work, Betsy. Christie shook hands with them all after their curtsies, which seemed to go down well. Zilpah stayed in the background but Christie introduced her, saying: 'Zilpah will help with anything, like she does at home.' Then, as they looked uneasily at her, she went on: 'You mustn't think she's different because she is black, you know. She is very kind and I have known her all my life. And would you please be patient with us as I think some words will be different in England to Charleston where we have come from, and I know we speak differently.'

'If I may say so, ma'am,' said Mrs Cardew, 'your accent is very attractive.' She looked at the others who nodded their heads vigorously. 'And we all welcome you both. I hope everything is to your liking.' She dismissed the staff and said: 'Please come this way and I will show you to your room, Miss Farrell. I have placed Zilpah in a small room opposite to yours as you may need her.'

Christie's room looked out on to the back of the house. There was a reasonable sized garden with trees where one could sit in the summertime. It could be very pleasant there, Christie thought. The trees now, though, were denuded of their leaves and the garden was without colour apart from some holly bushes with their red berries. 'It's the wrong time to visit,' thought Christie ruefully. 'Everything would look so much better during the summer months.'

The room seemed comfortable and the bed very inviting. The furniture was old but well polished and now the trunks were brought in, Zilpah came and helped Christie to unpack. Dresses were laid in the press, her smaller things in the chest of drawers. When everything was to Zilpah's satisfaction she returned to her own small but comfortable room.

That night Christie needed no sleeping draught to encourage her to enter the land of Nod. There were no voices shouting, no bells ringing, no being tossed on the high seas. As soon as her head was on the pillow she was away.

Consequently, the following morning when she awoke, which was quite late, she felt much better. She lay there thankful that at least the servants had been friendly on their arrival. She hoped Zilpah had slept well too. Perhaps everything would be all right after all and the more she thought about it the more optimistic she became. So that when a knock came on her door she was able to call out a cheery 'Come in,' as she sat up ready to receive her morning drink.

Bella opened the door calling, 'Good morning, Miss,' as she did so, carrying a small tray with a cup of chocolate and a biscuit. She approached the bed and her smiles turned to a look of horror. She stopped and her hands began to shake. 'Oh, Miss,' she panted. 'Your face.' Then she dropped the tray and rushed from the room.

Christie stared at the closing door in dismay. What had happened? Then she remembered her scar. She had forgotten about it as Zilpah usually saw her first in a morning. She felt and found she had pushed her hair away from her face as she used to do. She felt like weeping now. Did she look so terrible? Obviously she did as she had frightened Bella.

The door opened once more and Zilpah came in. 'I heard a noise, Miss Christie, what...?' She stopped as she saw the mess on the floor. 'Did you do dis, Miss Christie?'

Christie shook her head. 'No, Bella dropped it when she saw my—my face.' Her face crumpled then and sobs shook her. Zilpah hurried to put her arms around her.

'It's all right, Miss Christie, I'm here,' she crooned until the tears and sobs ceased. 'Now,' Zilpah said, 'I will fetch you more chocolate and I will see to de mess dat stupid Bella make. Let me tell dem how you got dat scar, Miss Christie. It will be best.'

'No, no Zilpah, please do not. They wouldn't understand and...no, please don't.'

Zilpah shrugged. 'Just as you say, Miss Christie, but I tink you wrong.' She disappeared with the empty cup and tray.

Christie mopped her face. She had felt so good when she'd woken up and now this!

Meanwhile, Zilpah had found the kitchen. She knocked on the door and entered to find Bella being comforted by Mrs Parsloe, the cook. Betsy was washing the dishes.

'Excuse me, ma'am. I come for Miss Farrell's hot chocolate if you please. Den I will clean de floor where it was spilled.' She plonked rather than placed the tray on the table.

'Very well,' said Mrs Parsloe, eyeing Zilpah, not knowing what to say. She went to pour more chocolate into another cup. Zilpah looked at Bella. 'Miss Farrell is sorry for de shock. You see dere was an accident and Miss Farrell now has scar.'

Bella swallowed and nodded but avoided Zilpah's eye.

'Go and clear up the mess, Betsy,' said Mrs Parsloe.

Zilpah smiled at Betsy and they went out together. Zilpah went into the room first followed by a frightened Betsy. But now Christie had placed her hair over the scar and had recovered herself.

'Why, Betsy,' she said. 'Thank you.' As the little maid set to work Christie went on: 'I think I have a new handkerchief in the drawer, Zilpah. Give it to Betsy if you please.'

Betsy looked up. 'Me, miss, but—but why?'

'Because you are cleaning up someone else's mess! Bella, I know, was frightened, but she should have come back and cleaned it up herself.'

'Please, Miss, is it true?' asked Betsy timidly.

'Is what true?'

'That you have been marked by the—the devil?' Betsy's eyes were large and round.

'Is that what they are saying? Well, of course it's not true. I had an accident, that is all.'

'Yes, Miss. Thank you for the handkerchief. I've never owned a proper one. I'll keep it for best.' Then she scuttled through the door while Christie thoughtfully supped her chocolate.

Later, downstairs, Christie noticed that they all avoided eye contact, even the housekeeper. Otherwise, they served her meals, answered her questions and were polite. Zilpah found the same when she entered the kitchen and they kept their distance.

The next day Christie decided that she and Zilpah would take a walk to the village. She found the Norman church of Saint Peter, which fascinated her as it was so old. In Charleston the churches were not such grand buildings or had such history. There was also a very busy hostelry where carriages came and went and weary travellers were set down.

Christie said: 'It is all so quaint and small, it is like a model.'

Some of the houses were of the previous century and some were thatched. After the open spaces of home this was all so different. She noticed a haberdasher's and saw through its tiny window a selection of ribbons and laces. After looking for a while she decided to go inside. She found the door locked.

'Oh, what a shame. Some of those pretty ribbons would be just what Carrie would like. Never mind, we'll try again another day.'

They tried another shop but it was closed too so they turned and visited the church which stood back off the road. They went under the lychgate, which Christie thought interesting, then followed the path to the door. Inside, the church was dim but the windows of stained glass would, on a sunny day, have sent forth rainbow coloured beams on to the boxed pews below. They spent a pleasant half hour looking at the windows and the carvings, which Christie thought quite beautiful and then they both sat in one of the wooden pews for a while, just being content to sit and look. Christie found the peace and quiet was very conducive to thinking.

As they came out she saw a lady enter the haberdasher's but when she tried the door again, it was locked. How odd! It was then that Christie came to the conclusion that it might be because Zilpah was black, which made her angry.

However, to prove this point, she asked Mary, Mrs Ford's dresser, if she would accompany her instead of Zilpah the next day. Mary, not liking this one little bit, demurred at first but seeing Christie's determination to go anyway, and alone if need be, she eventually agreed. They set off with Mary polite but hardly friendly. Christie sighed. There were more people about and Christie felt more optimistic about shopping but she found the villagers crossed the street in front of her or turned to look in a window rather than speak to her. Added to this the shopkeepers fastened their doors again when she and Mary approached. So in silence they returned to the house.

Christie took off her cloak and went up to her bedchamber. She was not comfortable using any of the other rooms. With Cousin Amelia not being there, she felt like an interloper and although she was sure the servants would not have objected initially, they would certainly object now. She sat down near the window to think. There was no use weeping anymore, she told herself, that would not solve the problem. What, though, was she to do? There was no one to whom she could turn. The only person she knew other than Zilpah and the servants was Mr Wicks, but he wasn't the kind of man one would open one's heart to. On a matter of law it would be different, perhaps, but who else was there? Perhaps someone at the church? The Vicar? Could she go to the door and ask to see him? She didn't know him so it would be hard to judge. However she could attend a service on the following Sunday and then decide if he could be of help. So that is what she resolved to do. If she could think of anything or anyone else in the meantime, that would be all to the good. She felt pleased that she could think about it all rationally now, as she did when she had problems at home. Evidently, her health was improving and, she told herself, she could cope.

She shivered, it was certainly colder and there was no fire in the grate. She decided to do something about it. She rang the bell. Little Betsy appeared, sniffing.

'Oh, Betsy, I have no fire.'

Betsy looked. 'No, Miss.' She looked hopefully at Christie.

'Well?' said Christie with a smile.

'Only fire is in the kitchen, Miss,' she sniffed again.

'I had better see Mrs Cardew then. I'll come down.'

She found Mrs Cardew in the hall. She was wearing a shawl. 'Mrs Cardew, it has turned very cold. Could a fire be lit in my room and Zilpah's, please?'

Mrs Cardew said slowly, 'I—I don't know, Miss. It costs a lot of money to have a lot of fires and I don't know whether Mr Wicks would allow it. It is a difficult situation and I don't know what I am supposed to do.'

'How many fires are alight in the house now?'

'Only the kitchen one, Miss, because of the cooking.'

'Of course. But we shall all die of cold if we don't keep warm, so if there is enough coal, please have everyone's fire lit. If not we must order more. If there is a problem with the money, I will have a word with Mr Wicks when he comes. I will foot the bill myself if necessary.'

'Thank you, Miss Farrell.' Mrs Cardew went off visibly pleased with this announcement and Christie felt better for having made a positive decision that was pleasing.

That night the weather became colder and warming pans were put in use to air and warm the beds. Christie slept well and awoke the following morning to a bright room, but there seemed something odd about it. Outside appeared to be very quiet and everywhere still. Surely she hadn't become deaf overnight? She listened hard now and could just make out a few sounds inside the house as the servants stirred. But why was it so different? She decided she must find out so she moved quickly over to the window and drew back the draperies. She couldn't believe her eyes. Everywhere was white. It had snowed in the night. She just stared. She had never seen anything quite like it. Zilpah knocked on the door and brought in her chocolate. When she saw Christie out of bed she said: 'Miss Christie, you'll catch your deat'. Get back into bed at once.'

'Zilpah, have you seen outside. Isn't it beautiful?'

'Uh-huh.' She stood waiting and Christie hurried up and slipped into her bed to have her drink.

'Shall we go out in it, Zilpah?'

'No, it too cold. We stay in de nice warm house.'

'Well, I shall go out by myself then. It will be good to have some air.'

By the time she had her hot chocolate, a bath, dressed and appeared in the breakfast room, the morning was much advanced. Christie looked out of the window once more. The garden looked so different. Everything was transformed into weird looking shapes by the snow. Christie changed into her walking shoes, put on her warm hood and cloak and prepared to depart. Zilpah said she was to be sure and return soon otherwise she would be frozen like the trees and bushes.

Christie took a deep breath and left the warmth of the house. The cold certainly hit her but she turned resolutely away from the village to walk where, hopefully, there were no people. The wind blew slightly and she held on to her cloak. After a little while she found a small lane. Either side were hedges with fields beyond, all coated in white. She had to watch where she placed her feet to avoid where the snow lay deepest. She looked back and saw her footprints, the first ones to be made in the pristine path. How Carrie and Charlotte would have enjoyed it! She could imagine them trying to push each other into the snow, squealing and laughing. She had not been able to walk as quickly as usual but she had kept up a reasonable pace. Now she was pleased to rest at a five-barred gate where she paused to catch her breath. She continued to think of them all at home and then wondered if it would be a good idea to return there soon. After all, there was nothing to keep her here, only the chance to see something of England while she had the opportunity. How could she do that though, with no chaperone to accompany her and tell her how to go on? She was deep in thought when she felt a definite nudge on her leg. Scared, she looked down quickly and gasped as a spaniel was looking up at her, wagging its tail.

'Oh,' she said with relief.

A soft voice was murmuring: '*I saw fair Chloris walk alone/Where feathered rain came softly down*'. Then rather more loudly the voice said, 'It's all right, Polly won't hurt you.'

Christie saw the figure of a man standing in the lane. He wore a long dark coat nearly reaching his feet and which had seen better days. On his head he had a large floppy brimmed hat, which Christie had seen workmen wear. Yet his voice was not that of a workman.

She patted Polly. 'Good morning, sir, I was faraway, I fear. I didn't notice your dog.'

He smiled and walked towards her. 'Were you looking at something interesting?' he asked.

'No, no. It—I was thinking.'

'Mm. It is rather cold to stand and think, isn't it? Wouldn't it be better to think where it's warm?'

'I suppose so but it was important, you see.'

'Oh. Well, walk back with me towards the village. It is rather overcast, you know and could snow again.'

She was aware of him watching her keenly from under the large brim of his hat but he didn't say any more.

'Perhaps it would be sensible to return. I feel chilly.'

'May I ask where you are staying?'

'Well,' said Christie, 'I came to visit Mrs Ford who lived in the house on the edge of the village. Unfortunately she died before I was able to meet her. I'm staying there just for the moment, though.'

'Ah.'

While they walked and talked, he kept an eye on Polly, who followed at her own pace, stopping now and again to nose at some object or to follow some interesting scent.

'Do you live in the village, sir?' Christie asked, trying to be friendly.

'Just outside,' he said but didn't elaborate. 'We go for a walk everyday, don't we, Polly?' he said to the spaniel as she caught up with them.

Christie had nearly retraced her steps when her companion stopped. 'You look very cold,' he said, looking at her pink tipped nose and white face. 'Would you join Polly and me at the little inn over there for a hot drink?'

She was by now very cold and she couldn't feel her fingers; also, she felt she had had enough and would like to sit down for a while. Perhaps she wasn't as strong as she thought, for her energy seemed to dwindle very quickly. The man waited patiently for her answer. She smiled wearily up at him.

'Very well, thank you,' she said.

Chapter 13

They entered the Lamb and Flag, which felt very warm and cosy. The landlord hurried forward to greet them saying what a shock the arrival of the snow had been.

'Could we be where it's quiet, please?' asked the gentleman.

'Of course, sir. Everywhere is empty at the moment. Not many folk will venture out for a while. The coffee room has a good fire, if the young lady would like to go in there.'

He led the way to a small oak beamed room where the fire dominated. Christie took off her cloak and went to sit next to the fire but her companion stopped her. 'You would be better here for a while,' he said pointing to a comfortable seat further away. 'We don't want you to be ill, do we? And you Polly,' he added, clicking his fingers so that the dog moved further back. She went to sit next to Christie while the gentleman took off his disreputable hat and coat. Underneath, he wore a plain dark green coat of very fine quality wool and long black boots. At his neck he wore a snowy white stock but his wavy hair was carelessly tied back. Christie felt she liked him in the worn topcoat best, he looked more approachable.

'Would you and the lady like some hot punch, sir?' asked the landlord.

'That would be wonderful, thank you. Polly, go with this good man and find a drink.' Polly went with the landlord, tail wagging.

Christie asked, 'What is punch, please?'

'A nice hot drink. You will soon see. But don't worry,' he said kindly. 'If you don't like it, you can have something else.'

'Thank you,' she said, remembering to check that her hair covered the scar. She didn't want to upset her companion.

He sat down opposite her. 'Are your feet wet? Take your shoes off if they are. And why aren't you wearing pattens?'

'Because I haven't any,' she said, slipping off her shoes but making sure her feet were out of sight under the folds of her dress.

'So, how long have you been in Stanton? And did you enjoy the Atlantic crossing?'

'Oh, I expect you can tell from my accent,' said Christie. 'And no, I didn't enjoy the crossing. It was long and boring really. And I have only been here just over a week.'

'I have been away myself. That is why I haven't met you before. And do you like it here?'

These questions were getting too close for comfort, so she prevaricated. 'I—I really haven't been here long enough to find out.'

'I see.'

She looked up at him. He smiled sweetly, his eyes (were they hazel?) looked kindly at her from under his dark brows. 'So why do you have to walk out on a cold morning to think? Is it such a problem?'

She had wanted someone to confide in and ask what she should do and here he was! Should she throw caution to the winds and tell him all, even though she had just met him? He looked so kindly at her now, but she found she could not do it. She didn't even know who he was and she didn't like to ask. It would be rash to be so trusting in one she had only just met. Good gracious, he might tell wild stories about her all over Stanton. But then, looking at him again, she did not think he would. Fortunately for her, the landlord came in then with the bowl of hot punch and proceeded to ladle it into two goblets.

'I'll leave it here, sir, in case you need more. Oh, I'll bring some of the special sweet biscuits my wife makes for the young lady. And Polly has a bone, sir,' he added as he disappeared again. Polly then made her appearance carrying a large marrow bone in her mouth. Her plume of a tail waved back and forth to tell everyone how pleased she was.

'Do you suppose you can chew it quietly?' asked her master.

Polly, hearing his voice, looked up and wagged her tail again before starting the enjoyable task of gnawing her gift.

Christie saw her companion dip his finger and thumb into his waistcoat pocket and bring out a silver container shaped like a small egg. He opened this, took out a tiny grater and proceeded to grate the nutmeg, which was in the lower part, on to the top of his drink. 'Would you like some of this, do you think?' he asked. 'Taste your drink first and see,' he suggested as Christie hesitated.

'Ooh! That tastes good. May I try…?'

He grated some nutmeg on the top of Christie's drink, after which he returned it to his pocket. Christie held the goblet with the warm liquid between both hands.

'Mm. It's lovely. Thank you, you are very kind to invite me.'

He acknowledged her with a nod but said, 'May I ask what this problem is? Maybe I can help?'

Christie looked into her punch for a moment. 'It's just that I wondered if I could go to Bristol while the snow was on the ground.' She said it in a rush and then looked up. The man was watching her, but said nothing, only frowned.

Christie flushed slightly. 'I would like to shop, you see. I—I need a muff or mittens.' The answer was only a half-truth, she knew, but it was difficult to tell the whole truth without revealing everything.

'I believe there are suitable shops here in Stanton. Why go to Bristol?' He sipped his drink but still kept his eyes on her.

'Yes, well, it—it isn't as easy as that.' A shade of bitterness crept into her voice.

'Oh? Tell me.'

Christie recovered herself. 'It is of no consequence, sir. I would not want to…'

'But I am intrigued. Why isn't it easy to buy those things in Stanton? The shops are perfectly good.'

'I'm sure they are, sir, but I am a stranger and I have found on two occasions that their doors are locked when I appear. And it is not because my servant is black,' she finished indignantly. She took a large mouthful of her drink and choked slightly as she swallowed. She did not see the twitching lips of the gentleman in front of her. When he thought she had recovered a little he said: 'I find this very interesting. Have you any idea why they should do this? I do not believe it is because you are from South Carolina and your accent is different. In fact, your voice is very melodic and the accent very attractive, you know. There must be another reason, mustn't there?'

Christie looked up and nodded, saying slowly, 'Yes, there is, of course, but I didn't really want to—to tell you.'

'I see. Of course, that is up to you. I will not force your confidence but if you would like to tell me any time, I will listen, you know.'

'Thank you, you are very kind.' Christie answered so softly he could hardly hear her.

He was really curious but he also realised this girl was very unhappy and as far as he could make out, completely on her own apart from a black servant. What a pity he had been away when she had arrived. Now how could he gain her confidence and help her? Why did he wish to help her? He thought perhaps it was because there was a mystery attached to her? Also, he thought she was very pretty, from what he could see of her face, which added to the attraction. He sipped his drink, watching her.

Christie, aware of his regard, adjusted her hair, thinking he might glimpse her dreaded scar. She would be loath to disgust him with her looks after he had been so kind to her.

'What I find difficult to understand is why you visit England at the worst time of the year. If you had waited a few more months you would be here for the Spring, which is very pleasant, you know. Or did you hope to see Mrs Ford before she died?'

'No, we didn't know she was ill. She is my Father's cousin. I did not know her at all.'

'And whereabouts do you live in Carolina with your Father?'

'Charleston, sir. My Father owns a cotton plantation, you see. We have a large house and I am the eldest of four daughters. Sadly, Mama died two years ago.' Christie now felt on safer ground and happily told him about Charleston, the girls and the slaves.

He listened intently, never taking his eyes off her. When she had finished, he said: 'What a lively and busy life you must lead. It makes me wonder even more, why you come here at this time.' He raised his eyebrows as he spoke.

Christie licked her lips. 'Well, you see, I had an accident and it was thought a good idea for me to go away for a while. So I came here.'

'Dear me, I'm sorry about that. It must have been serious to go to such lengths.'

Christie shrugged. 'I suppose so,' she said quietly.

Her companion ladled a little more punch into her goblet. He thought he could not press her any further. Obviously the whole episode had been, and still was, painful for her. Maybe she would tell him all in the future when she knew him better. He would just have to wait and see. He intended to see her again if at all possible.

'Now let me tell you a little about Stanton and what goes on around here. If the weather becomes really cold and icy the large pond in the village freezes and there is skating. Do you skate?' When she shook her head he went on: 'Well, that is something to learn if you feel so inclined, it is great fun. The people are quite a social lot really. I know you haven't seen any of it yet but it can be remedied. There are dances and parties and invitations to each other's houses to drink tea and hear music. Then when the Spring comes and the weather is milder there is the Spring Fair. There are plenty of young ladies in the village who are friendly, you know.' He favoured Christie with his sweet smile.

Christie looked at him. He was being so kind and trying to be helpful but she still felt she could not confide in him just yet. So she smiled in return and said: 'It all sounds wonderful and I'm sure when I have been here a little longer, I shall find it just as you say.'

'Well, we had better go. Your servant will wonder where you are and will be coming in search of you.' He hesitated to say more as Christie had moved and he saw the mark on the lower part of her face. Her problem was something to do with that mark? He thought quickly and instead of getting up he said: 'But before we go, I want to tell you something.'

Christie looked up, putting her hand immediately on her hair. 'Yes?'

'It is an allegory. Do you like allegories? It goes like this.' He had to make it up as he went along so he hoped it would work. 'A young girl worked in a castle. One day she was told to clean one of the rooms. The room had two doorways. One had a curtain over it, the other showed a skeleton sitting on a chair. At first, the maid was frightened of the skeleton but then she became accustomed to it sitting there and eventually she was able to clean the room without bothering about it. The doorway with the curtain, however, became more of a nightmare as she didn't know what lay behind it and she imagined all kinds of horrible things. But when the curtain was drawn back she found only an empty chair.'

Before Christie could say anything her companion had risen and went in search of the landlord. Not knowing what to think she hurriedly put on her dry shoes and her cloak, making sure the hood was in place. Had he guessed her problem? It was obvious he was not stupid. Would she regret joining him just now? She had enjoyed being with him and drinking punch but would the tale be all round Stanton after this? Somehow she did not seem to care!

He returned and donned his hat and coat. Polly, seeing him ready to go, carried her bone over to him and dropped it at his feet.

'Well?' he asked. 'What's that for?'

Polly picked up the bone and dropped it again, looking up at him and wagging her tail.

'I thought so. You want me to carry it? All right, as I have my old coat on, I will, but I don't promise to carry your bones in the future.' He picked up the half chewed bone between thumb and finger and dropped it into his pocket. 'Ugh,' he said. Polly wagged her tail and went to the door.

They thanked the landlord and Christie gasped as she went outside, it seemed even colder.

'It's because we've been so warm. Come along, a sharp walk and you'll soon be back indoors.'

Christie felt a little light-headed. Was it the cold or too much punch? After thanking her companion for his hospitality she confined her efforts to walking and breathing. It wasn't long before she was back at Mrs Ford's house. She knocked on the door and Zilpah opened it immediately. Meanwhile, the man, tipping his hat with a murmured 'Good day Miss Farrell,' went on his way, followed by tail wagging Polly.

Chapter 14

'It lunchtime, Miss Christie,' said Zilpah by way of greeting and eyeing her young mistress as Christie hurried into the house, taking off her cloak as she did so. She gave a big sigh.

'Is it, Zilpah? I lost count of the time.' She climbed the stairs slowly as her head was swimming a little. It felt quite pleasant, really. She smiled to herself. The walk in the snow had been good for her. The meeting with the gentleman was just by the way. She went over it all again in her mind and had just reached her room when she realised what he had said on departure. Now, how had he known her name? She sat on the side of the bed, frowning. She was sure she had not told him. Then she saw herself in the mirror and remembered the story he had told her. She took her comb and parted her hair like she used to and tied it in a ribbon. Her scar showed, of course, but was it not so bad, after all? Perhaps it was right what the gentleman had said about covering things up. If she had shown the scar from the outset, then it wouldn't have been such a shock to Bella. She tidied herself and went down to lunch, her head held high.

The following day she received a letter from Mr Wicks saying that he would visit at the earliest opportunity and would like the staff to be present. Christie, guessing that it was about Mrs Ford's will, told Mrs Cardew who said she would see that everyone was told.

Fortunately no more snow fell and the weather became slightly warmer. Therefore it began to melt which made walking difficult but at least the coaches could now be used again. So it was two days after Christie had received the letter from Mr Wicks that that gentleman arrived. He saw the staff first as they had all been mentioned in Mrs Ford's will and each had been left a small amount of money, even little Betsy. As Christie had refused to attend this meeting as she said that it had nothing to do with her, she was now requested by Mr Wicks to join them.

'I have to tell you all that as some of you may know, Mrs Ford had a sister, Mrs Bush. She, with her son, will be on their way from Yorkshire as I speak, to visit. This house, together with the remainder of the money, has been left to them. They will be here in a day or two. Perhaps you will be good enough to see to the preparations, Mrs Cardew?'

'Yes sir. Could I ask, for all of us, will they be living here permanently eventually, do you know sir? If so, will she need us or shall we begin looking for other positions?'

'Now that I do not know, I'm afraid, at the moment. You will have to wait and see.'

Christie cleared her throat. 'There will hardly be room for Mrs Ford's sister and her son with their servants, sir, if Zilpah and I are still in the house. I think, perhaps, it would be better if we moved out into a house of our own. Could you help me with that, do you think, or tell me to whom I must go?'

Mr Wicks looked at her and smiled. 'Thank you, Miss Farrell, you have made my work easier. I can certainly help you but I'm afraid I cannot find a house straightaway, before Mrs Bush arrives, that is. But certainly I will do my best.'

'Thank you,' said Christie. 'I am much obliged to you, Mr Wicks. Then I can tell Mrs Bush that we will be moving a soon as possible when she arrives. It must look very odd to have someone living here who is hardly any relation.'

Mr Wicks said, 'I'm sure she will understand the situation and I did my best to explain it in the letter.' He then departed, leaving, as was natural, uneasiness among the servants.

Before the servants left the room Christie stood up in front of them. 'Could I please have your attention for a moment.' They all stood there waiting, not meeting her eyes. 'It is just that I would like to apologise to you all about the—the scar on my face, and especially to Bella. I should not have covered it up in the first place and then it wouldn't have been such a shock. I cannot tell you the full story, I'm afraid, because it involves other people, but I was unfortunate enough to be in the way when someone was using a whip. It caught my back and, as you see, my face. I am well now, but that is why I came over here for a—a change of scene. I hope now that you will get used to seeing me like this for the short time I shall be in this house.' By the time she had finished, her voice was shaking and she had to bite her lip and swallow hard to stop the tears from falling. The truth still hurt, evidently. She fervently hoped she would soon overcome it.

Mrs Cardew was the first to speak. 'Oh, Miss Farrell, how dreadful for you—and I shall speak for all of us when I say how sorry we are. You see, Miss, we live in a village and villagers are very superstitious about anything they don't understand. Now we do, it will be all right.'

'Thank you,' said Christie.

The staff filed out, which gave Christie the opportunity to have a word with Mrs Cardew, suggesting that if it was of any help, Zilpah could share her room. Mrs Cardew said it would not be necessary to add to Miss Farrell's inconvenience. Over the following days Christie noticed that the servants treated her once again with respect as when she had first arrived and even accepted how she looked without dropping their eyes. Christie realised she felt much happier. She was looking forward to having her own house and she might even find people friendlier.

She was about to go to her room when Mary saw her and nervously asked if she could have a word. Christie nodded and led the way into the morning room.

'What is it, Mary?' Christie asked as she sat down.

'Miss Farrell, could I please ask you something?'

'Of course.'

'I—I'm sorry that I treated you badly, going to the shops, I mean. Since Mr Wicks's visit, I've been thinking, and I wondered if you would want a dresser when you move. You see, I expect Mrs Bush has her own, but if you want someone I could work for you. But I expect you wouldn't want me?'

Poor Mary by this time was twisting her hands and looking decidedly uncomfortable. Christie smiled slightly and drew a chair forward. 'Sit down, Mary.' Mary sat, albeit on the edge.

'Now,' said Christie, 'we will forget about my face and our trip to the shops. What we have to think of is a position for you. I am in England for only a short while, I think. I haven't even thought much about it, as there have been other things on my mind. However, I would be quite happy for you to help me with my clothes as I need to buy some more and you will know just where I am to go. So why don't you come to me and stay while I am here and I will let you know in good time when I plan to return home, so that you could find a new position. How does that sound?'

'Oh, Miss, that will be just right, thank you. I was so worried.'

'Very well, Mary. Thank you.' As the door closed Christie smiled to herself. She just hoped Mrs Bush wasn't in need of a dresser.

The next day Christie decided to visit the shops again. She had now regained some of her usual determination so with a firm step and accompanied by Zilpah she once more tried the shop doors. This time there were no problems whatsoever, the ladies behind the counters nearly bending over backwards to serve her. Finally, after spending some time looking and buying, Christie managed to carry home all the purchases which included ribbons for Carrie, mittens and a muff and also pattens for herself and Zilpah in case of more inclement weather. She did wonder at the change of attitude of the shopkeepers towards her and vaguely wondered if someone had said anything on her behalf. Was it the gentleman she had met down the lane? And if so, what standing did he have in the village that he could alter things to that extent? Perhaps though, he had none whatsoever and she was just under a misapprehension.

There was still no sign of Mrs Bush and her son. Christie wondered if the weather conditions in the north were much worse than in the south or if they had another reason for not travelling, as they still did not appear. Preparations had been made for them, with meals prepared in case they arrived, but they still did not reach Stanton. Christie felt pleased as she hoped to be on the verge of moving out or even moved before they finally came.

What did come, however, was an invitation to take tea with a Mrs Henshaw at Langley Manor the following afternoon. To Mary's delight, Christie sent for her to ask what gown she considered suitable for such an occasion, as at home it was so different. Mary suggested something plain and subdued, saying that although Miss did not know Mrs Ford, it would look odd to wear something too bright after her death, and especially as Miss Farrell was living in her house. So in the end they settled for a plain blue silk gown, shot with grey, with fine lace at the elbows and neckline. Mary said the blue enhanced Miss Farrell's eyes. Zilpah was to accompany her as Mary said Mrs Henshaw was a well-known lady, as she lived at the manor house just outside Stanton. Everything had to be just right.

So on the following afternoon, Mrs Ford's small carriage was at the door in time to take Christie and Zilpah, who were warmly dressed in cloaks and hoods, to Langley Manor.

It lay to the south of Stanton so the carriage with Christie and Zilpah inside had to travel the length of the village, then along a road that eventually branched off to the drive leading to the house. As far as Christie could see, the drive was tree lined, she thought by oaks, and various coniferous bushes. There were still small patches of snow here and there and muddy areas where it had melted, as well as mounds of blackened leaves that had been left to rot since their fall in the autumn, making the earth rich as they composted.

In a matter of minutes they stopped outside a heavy oaken doorway and Christie could see the manor was very old. It looked interesting, she thought, and she particularly liked the mellow stonework. How old was this porch, she wondered? But there was no time to stand and stare as the door opened and they stepped inside.

A footman took them to a large panelled hall where Christie's cloak was taken. There was a large stone fireplace but she was surprised to see there was no fire here in welcome. When she asked where Zilpah could stay the footman indicated a seat there.

'Will you be all right, Zilpah? Keep your cloak on. I'll try not to be too long,' she whispered.

'It all right, Miss Christie. I's fine.' She nodded and Christie followed the footman who led her up the oaken staircase to the drawing room, where she was announced.

The room Christie entered was in contrast to the hall. It was warm with a roaring fire in the grate and many candles were already alight. A small elderly lady, her white hair dressed high, probably to make her appear taller, came towards her. She supported herself with an ebony cane.

'Welcome, Miss Farrell. I'm Mrs Henshaw.'

Christie curtseyed. 'How kind of you to invite me to take tea with you,' she said.

'Now,' said Mrs Henshaw, 'there are some young ladies over there whom I'm sure you would like to talk to. Ladies,' she called, rapping her ebony cane on the floor to make herself heard above their chatter, 'this is Miss Farrell.'

'Oh,' answered one of the young ladies, 'do join us, Miss Farrell.' So Christie went over and sat on the sofa in the centre of the group. They made a pretty picture in their silk dresses of various colours and patterns all with very much lace apparent and in most cases with quite low necklines. Their hair, mainly fair or powdered, was in varying styles from the simple mass of curls and ringlets to higher padded shapes. Long curls were in evidence, either natural or helped with the tongs. All were decorated with ribbons or jewelled clasps. Christie felt her dark hair, well brushed and tied simply with ribbons and draped over one shoulder, was not quite the thing but she consoled herself that her silk dress and lace were of the finest quality.

Mrs Henshaw had walked slowly back to a group of older ladies who, Christie supposed, were some of the young ladies' mamas. Probably the others had servants of some kind to accompany them although they were not apparent in the hall. As Christie sat, a footman brought her a cup of tea that her hostess had poured. She took it with a word of thanks. The other young ladies looked at each other and giggled.

'Tell us,' said one, 'where you come from. You speak differently.'

'I have come over from the Americas. I live in Charleston with my family.'

'I have heard that people are very poor over there,' said another, in a superior voice.

'Well,' said Christie, 'I suppose it is like everywhere else, there are poor people and those who are more affluent.' She sipped her tea.

'And which group do you come from?' laughed another.

One young lady said severely, 'Louisa, you cannot ask questions like that. What will Miss Farrell answer? If she says she is poor, we shall not want to know her. If she says she is rich, she won't want to know us.'

They all giggled.

The superior voiced one tried again. 'I hear there are people called Indians living in the Americas and they wear feathers and are fierce.'

The girls laughed. 'What frights they must look,' one said.

'I have yet to see them,' said Christie. 'They don't live near Charleston but those that are nearest are the Cherokees, I think. They are farming people and if left alone are no trouble.'

Then Christie tried to change the subject. 'Do you all live around Stanton?'

'Oh, yes,' drawled one. 'It is such a bore. I'd rather stay in Bath.'

'Why is that?' asked Christie. 'I've never been there.'

'Oh, dear,' said Louisa. 'Someone tell her.'

'It is a fashionable place where one can drink the waters, you know, for health. I don't think it would do anything for you, though. What do you think, ladies?'

'But I am perfectly healthy,' Christie said.

'But, my dear, your face,' remarked another.

Christie looked down into her cup, while silence reigned until Louisa said, 'Oh, come over to the window, all of you, I want to show you something.' She laughed as they all followed except Christie. She could hear them whispering and giggling.

Christie sipped more tea.

Meanwhile, Zilpah left in the hall, began to feel colder. She wiggled her toes endeavouring to keep them warm. She looked about her with interest but she dare not walk around in case someone saw her. In fact, now that she looked, she noticed a footman standing by the stairs. She wondered if he had been told to watch her in case she touched anything. While she sat there, all of a sudden the large outer door opened and a man came in. He stamped his feet and then proceeded to remove his tricorne and cloak. The footman moved forward to take them.

'Where's Perkins?'

'It's his afternoon off sir,'

'Really?' Then he noticed Zilpah, who had risen. He looked at the empty fireplace. 'Good God, why isn't the fire lit?'

'Mrs Henshaw said not to,' answered the footman flatly.

The man stiffened. He took out his snuffbox, his gaze not leaving the footman's face. 'Tell me,' he asked, his voice now soft and deadly, 'my memory cannot be as good as it used to be, but whose house is this?' He stared unblinkingly at the footman.

The poor fellow in front of him blenched. 'But—but it's yours, sir.'

'Quite so,' he now raised his voice. 'And I ordered *all* fires to be lit. See to it.' His eyes blazed. Zilpah, watching from the shadows, quaked in her shoes, but could not help but admire the man. He turned to her. She dropped him a small curtsey. He smiled a particularly sweet smile at her.

'You have been waiting in the cold. I am so sorry. You came with Miss Farrell, I expect.'

'Yessir.'

'Quite so.' He pulled the bell pull by the fireplace. Another footman appeared. 'Take this lady to Cook where it is warm and tell her to supply her with a hot drink. She is to stay until sent for.' He turned away, then back again and as an afterthought, said, 'Oh, perhaps she would like to talk to Toby?'

'Yes, sir. This way please.'

The man nodded to Zilpah and smiled again, somewhat slyly. Zilpah dropped another small curtsey and followed the footman.

The gentleman then went leisurely up the stairs and opened the door quietly where Mrs Henshaw was giving her tea party. He saw the older ladies having a good gossip, the young ladies giggling as usual over by the window and Miss Farrell sitting sedately drinking tea on her own. No one had heard his arrival. Once more the snuff-box was in evidence and although his voice was soft, it somehow seemed to cut through the feminine voices.

'And how is it that a new guest in *my house* is left on her own?'

The reactions of the drawing room inhabitants were a picture to behold. If the gentleman had a sense of humour he could not fail to, at least, applaud the reactions. The older ones stopped their gossip to stare at him open mouthed. The younger ones sat up straighter and after their initial surprise fixed smiles upon their faces and began to tweak their gowns into place or stroke a wayward curl.

Christie looked up surprised, recognising the soft voice of the gentleman who had bought her the punch in the Lamb and Flag. He now bowed slightly to the two groups of ladies and strode over to where Christie sat. Her cup, which she was holding in mid-air, she hastily returned to its saucer, which she placed on the table at her elbow. She rose to curtsey as the gentleman bowed.

'Miss Farrell, how nice to see you again. May I?' He indicated the seat next to hers.

'Of course. I…'

'Would you like more tea?' He clicked his fingers and two more cups of tea were brought.

'Now, how are you? You look better since I saw you last.' He smiled over his teacup.

'Thank you, sir. I am. Sir, is this indeed your house?'

'I believe so,' he answered, raising his eyebrows.

'Forgive me. You see, no one has told me anything since I have been here. From what I have seen, it looks a very beautiful house. And it was kind of your Mama to invite me…'

He interrupted. 'My Aunt. She lives here too. You see she had nowhere to live after her house had to be sold. So I gave her a home.'

'That was kind.'

He shrugged. 'Not really. There is plenty of room here as you can see, so it is no hardship for me. The only thing is she sometimes forgets it is my house and not hers and gives the servants orders she shouldn't. Hence no fire lit in the hall. That is now remedied and I had your servant taken down to Cook for a hot drink and company.'

Christie gave him a lovely warm smile. 'Oh, thank you. I was a little worried about leaving her there. Zilpah has been with our family for years and is a treasure. So thank you, Mr…? It can't be Henshaw, can it?'

'Sorry. How remiss of me. The name's Allard. Martin Allard.'

'Thank you, Mr Allard.'

'I see you have altered your hair. It looks much better like that, you know, and your face is more beautiful.' He said it in the same matter-of-fact voice and Christie was a second or two before she had realised what he had said. As she bowed her head and smiled, he went on: 'And how are the shops? Have you managed to buy anything yet or will you still go to Bristol?'

'Zilpah and I had a lovely time shopping and everyone was very friendly and kind. I wonder at the change but as it's for the better I must not complain.'

'No indeed.'

She looked suspiciously at him but he looked blandly back at her.

'Sir?'

'Madam?'

Christie laughed. 'Mr Allard, then. It is very kind of you to sit and talk to me, but shouldn't you be…?' She indicated the other groups of ladies.

'Are you teaching me etiquette, Miss Farrell?'

'No, no, I beg your pardon.'

He grinned. 'There is no need. You see, if I ignore them, perhaps they will learn to be more considerate of someone who is new to the country, in future.' This was said in a slightly louder voice than usual. Consequently, the young ladies bit their lips and made moues at each other and shrugged. They continued their conversations after that in monotones. The older ladies ignored him.

He turned his attentions back to Christie. 'So what are your plans now?'

'I have heard that Mrs Ford's sister and her son are coming down from Yorkshire. Whether they will stay permanently I do not know. But I have said that I will move to a house of my own, if possible, as it will be easier for everyone, I think. Mrs Ford's lawyer is looking for a place for me.'

Mr Allard nodded his head. 'I think you are wise. And, forgive me, do you have enough funds over here to cope with it all? If not, let me know.'

'That is very kind,' said Christie. 'I should be all right, my Father said he would make arrangements.'

'Good. But if there is a problem of any kind just tell me. I must go now. As you rightly say, I should have a word with the other guests otherwise I shall appear as rag-mannered as they are. It is nearly time for them to depart anyway.' He stood up. 'Thank you for coming, Miss Farrell. It was quite an ordeal for you, wasn't it?'

Christie nodded. He understood her feelings perfectly. 'Thank you,' she said. 'For—for everything.'

He bowed. 'A pleasure,' he said. 'And may I suggest a visit to Mrs Larkin might be of benefit to you? Everyone knows where she lives.' He nodded and pulled the bellcord, then joined the young ladies. When he was among them they all called to Christie: 'Bye, Miss Farrell, we hope to see you again.'

Christie smiled and curtseyed, then said her goodbyes to Mrs Henshaw.

CHAPTER 15

▼

On the way home Christie asked Zilpah if she had been looked after well.

'Oh, yes Miss Christie. I was cold wi' no fire but Mis' Allard said I was to go to da cook. She nice lady and I had hot wine. Very good. Did you like Mis' Allard, Miss Christie?'

'Yes, Zilpah. To me he was very kind but I feel if there was something he didn't like, he wouldn't hesitate to say so.'

'He good to me too. I liked him.'

'Oh, he said I was to visit a Mrs Larkin.'

'What for?'

'I don't really know but I think it is to do with my—my face.'

'Uh-huh,' replied Zilpah.

However, when Christie asked little Betsy who Mrs Larkin was, her eyes opened wide. 'Oh, Miss,' she said, 'she's a witch.'

'A witch?' laughed Christie. 'She cannot be. Why would she be a witch, Betsy?'

'Well,' said Betsy, nervously licking her lips, 'she has a black cat and she grows plants and she speaks ever so sharply. She "sees" people, too.'

Christie laughed. 'There are a lot of people like that, Betsy. Does she have a broomstick?'

'I don't know Miss. She could have.'

'I think I must go and see her. Where does she live?'

'She has a little cottage. But Miss, you will be careful? Look, you can borrow this if you like.' She took a cheap necklace from her pocket on which hung what looked like a small piece of coral.

'What is it?' asked Christie.

'It's solid blood of Jesus Christ. It will protect you from witchcraft.'

Christie smiled. 'Thank you, but I might lose it. You keep it safe. I shall be all right.'

Betsy went on to tell Christie how to find Mrs Larkin's house. It was outside the village, evidently standing alone beside the woodlands.

So the following morning Christie decided to have a walk. She wrapped up warmly and was just going to set off when Zilpah reminded her she should not go alone.

'No one will see me. It is only a village and Mrs Larkin is probably just an old lady. I am not bound by convention here and if I am I shall dispense with it for once, Zilpah.'

Zilpah shrugged. 'All right, Miss Christie, but I should go wi' you.'

'Zilpah, it is still freezing outside. You will be ill. I move quickly so I'll go alone. If I'm not back by lunchtime then send out someone to find me. Mind you, if Mrs Larkin is a witch, I may have been turned into something else.' She laughed mischievously as the door closed.

Christie set off at a good pace and after twenty minutes' walking came to a lane that led to the woods. She had passed few people on this cold morning but those she had seen all spoke to her. She felt a sense of belonging now. Eventually she saw a tiny cottage with a garden surrounding it. She stood and looked over the small hedge. It was all tidy and neat. No doubt in the spring, new plants and flowers would emerge. The cottage was thatched and very small. She knocked on the door.

A voice called, 'Come in. The door is unlatched.'

So Christie entered. 'Mrs Larkin?' she asked.

She found a little lady dressed in black with a white lace cap on her head. She was sitting by the fire, knitting.

'Come in and get warm,' she said.

'Thank you,' said Christie, 'I'm...'

'Miss Farrell? I know. Have you brought Zilpah with you?'

'No, but how did you...?'

'How did I know? I hear things and I remember.' She laid down her needles, her lined face creased in smiles. Bright blue eyes looked at Christie.

'M'mm,' she said, 'you've suffered with that, m'dear, haven't you?' She indicated Christie's scar.

'Well, at first, now it is just—just an eyesore, isn't it?'

Mrs Larkin looked, considering it, with her head to one side like an inquisitive sparrow. 'No, I don't think so but it can be improved. Would you like some cream to rub into it at night? It would help, you know. Let me show you.'

If Mrs Larkin was an older lady, she didn't show it as she jumped up out of her little armchair and scurried out of the room with great speed. While she was gone, Christie saw a large black cat coming towards her. It moved slowly and sedately, then sat in front of Christie, looking at her out of sleepy green eyes.

'No, Tommy,' said Mrs Larkin, coming back into the room. 'Miss Farrell doesn't want a big lump like you on her lap.'

Christie stroked the cat; he purred and settled down in front of the fire.

A jar was handed to Christie. She took off the top and gingerly sniffed it. There was a faint perfume but nothing unpleasant. 'It is made from an infusion of comfrey leaves, oil from the calendulas, beeswax and other things which I have in my garden. It helps to renew the skin and is equally good for chapped hands.'

'It sounds good and smells nice,' said Christie.

'Take it and try it. I don't promise miracles, you know, but it could help if you persevere with it.'

'Thank you. Could I take another jar for the servants, do you think? Poor little Betsy has to wash the dishes and her little hands are so red as a result.'

'You have a kind heart, Miss Farrell.' For some reason Mrs Larkin seemed to be pleased, Christie thought, but perhaps it was just that she was selling two jars of cream instead of one.

'Now before you go, how about a hot drink? I make my own tea out of herbs. This one has a little honey in to sweeten it.'

Christie thanked her and said she would love to try it. Mrs Larkin fetched the necessary china and poured boiling water into the teapot from the kettle that sat on the hob by the fire. While Christie waited for her tea she looked round and saw how clean and tidy everywhere was and no sign at all of witchcraft as far as she could see. It was all a lot of nonsense.

The tea was poured. 'Taste it and see what you think,' said Mrs Larkin.

Christie sipped her tea. It was an acquired taste but quite pleasant for all that. Mrs Larkin watched Christie and smiled saying, 'No dear. I'm not a witch although people think I am.'

Christie was a little disconcerted. 'I'm sorry,' she began.

'Don't be. How could you understand? But shall I explain it to you? Then you can believe me or not. Most people in the village will not try to understand so therefore think I'm a witch. In previous years other poor souls have been burnt at the stake for having gifts like mine. Sometimes now, it can still happen or they are ducked in the pond. I have to be careful, that is why I live here alone.'

'But what are these gifts? Do please explain to me. I am very interested.'

'Well, I think my senses are very acute as I can tell what most people are thinking, but not all the time, of course. I can also tell if there is a problem like illness. I could tell as soon as you walked in that you had been ill, apart from seeing the scar. But don't worry, things will change eventually for you.'

'Really? That is very nice to know. Thank you. And is there anything else you are able to do?'

'Oh yes,' said Mrs Larkin. 'Perhaps you won't believe me but I can see people who have died. Not everyone, of course, but I can see the couple who used to live here, for instance. They walk around but they never bother me. There is a pretty young lady who appears in the garden from time to time. They are all harmless. If I went elsewhere I should probably see others but I don't travel around very much now. It isn't frightening at all as I've always been used to it. It is a gift but others think it strange.'

'Are you lonely?'

'Oh, no, dear, not now. Life was hard when I was younger but I have been fortunate to find Mr Allard who is very good to me. He has one of his servants deliver my groceries for me and he visits me from time to time. So does the Vicar. I am happy.' She smiled at Christie. 'And so will you be eventually.'

'May I come again?'

'Any time you like, dear. I shall be pleased to see you.'

Then Christie said goodbye to Mrs Larkin.

'Later in the year, you can come and see the bees at work in the hives. They love it here with all the herbs and flowers.'

Christie thanked her and wondered on her walk back if she would still be in Stanton later in the year. She thought she might be. At the moment she had a sense of well-being. Was it because of Mrs Larkin's herb tea?

However, the sense of well-being deserted her when she arrived back at the house. It was in turmoil as Mrs Bush and her son had arrived. The hall was cluttered with trunks, cases, cloaks and shawls. Mrs Cardew was talking to a large lady, or at least, listening to her. When she saw Christie she hastened to introduce her. Mrs Bush turned. She had a superior look on her heavy, dark, face, as though there was a nasty smell somewhere. Her lips were straight and uncompromising.

'Oh, there you are,' she said. She looked Christie up and down. 'I thought you would have been here to greet us.' She sniffed.

'I may have done so if I had known you were arriving this morning, Ma'am,' said Christie.

'Good gracious, you speak English in a funny way,' frowned Mrs Bush.

'So do you,' Christie flashed back at her. Actually Mrs Bush spoke with a definite Yorkshire accent. Having married a Yorkshireman and living in Yorkshire, that was no wonder, of course. Christie did not object to different regional accents, she found them interesting, but it was Mrs Bush's attitude that annoyed her.

Christie tried again. 'Did you have a good journey, Mrs Bush?'

'Huh! No, we didn't. It was cold and dismal…'

She was interrupted by a young man who came towards them from the dining room. He positively strutted. He was of a stocky build and walked with a definite air of self-confidence. He was rather rotund, and even his light blue eyes looked round in his plump, fair face. His hair was straight and tied back firmly in the nape of his neck 'Good morning,' he said. 'You must be Miss Farrell who Mr Wicks told us about?'

Christie acknowledged him with a slight curtsey.

'Good morning, Mr Bush. You are correct.'

'You still live here then?'

'Just at the moment, but I shall move out as soon as Mr Wicks finds me a house.'

Zilpah came hurrying in to take Christie's cloak and bonnet.

'Good gracious! Who is that?' Mrs Bush stared aghast at Zilpah.

'This is Zilpah. She came over from Charleston with me,' said Christie, ready to do battle on Zilpah's behalf.

'Keep her away from us. She's heathen.'

'Don't worry, Zilpah would not want to be anywhere near you. Come Zilpah.'

Christie ran up the stairs to her room followed more slowly by Zilpah. She sat on her bed, fuming. 'Oh, Zilpah, they are horrid and I felt so happy this morning for some reason or other. Now they have spoilt it all.'

Zilpah laughed. 'You must expect it, Miss Christie. You know we are different.'

'I would have liked to have—have punched her on the nose,' finished Christie in a rush. 'Oh, let us hope we can move soon.'

'How did you find the witch?' asked Zilpah, tactfully changing the subject.

'Mrs Larkin's no witch, just a clever little lady. She gave me this cream to put on my face at night. There is a pot for the servants too, especially for little Betsy to use. Take it down with you when you go and tell her about it.'

'What will you do now?'

'Stay out of the way, I think. It's all right Mr Allard saying everyone is nice really. Those two are going to be trouble. I can feel it. And those girls whom I met at the Manor were very rude. If Papa had heard any of us behaving in such a manner we would be sent to our rooms with a severe scold.'

Zilpah laughed. 'Oh, Miss Christie, you frowning. It not good for your face.'

'I don't care about my face any more,' went on her rebellious mistress.

'You have nice face,' placated Zilpah.

Perforce, Christie had to go down to lunch. She could not ask for it to be sent up to her room, as the servants were so busy. However, it was not so bad as she expected. Mrs Bush said very little, leaving most of the talking to her son, Milton. Christie judged he was in his thirties although he seemed much older. His face would have been quite pleasant if he had not been so serious. Christie thought him pompous.

'The journey was tedious,' he said.

'It was a long way to come in this weather,' contributed Christie.

Then he proceeded to tell her about the countryside of the various counties they had passed through, and where they stayed and what it was like. It was a dry monologue, and Christie endeavoured to break the monotony of the flow by making suitable remarks about Stanton. But he ignored her and carried on while Christie's eyes glazed over and she said no more. She just concentrated on her food.

When the ordeal was over she excused herself and retired to her room again. However was she to manage at dinnertime? Perhaps they would eat as quickly as they had at lunch—then she could leave them as soon as dinner was over. She did not look forward to it, or the probable indigestion!

The following morning Christie had her breakfast alone and resolved to go out immediately afterwards and keep out of the way of Milton Bush and his mother. She thought she would visit the shops and the church again or she could find another lane to walk down and explore. So after a word with Zilpah and Mary, she put on her bonnet and donned her cloak and was just opening the door when the voice of Milton called: 'Miss Farrell, wait.' For the sake of politeness, Christie hesitated. Afterwards, she wished she had turned a deaf ear.

'Good morning, Mr Bush,' was all she said, still poised at the door.

'You must have someone to accompany you, you know. Wait one moment and it will be my pleasure.'

'But not mine,' thought Christie. She did not know what to do so she went outside and began to walk. Milton Bush could catch her up if he were that keen. She heard him puffing behind her.

'You walk very quickly. Where are you going?'

'I'm taking some exercise and it is cold. Therefore I walk quickly,' she said.

'Where are you going?'

'I'll go with you,' he said simply.

So Christie decided to find the lane where she first met Mr Allard and Polly. As the snow had gone now, maybe she could walk along further. Milton Bush began to talk but Christie ignored him. He went on for such long periods that she lost the thread of what he was saying. So she concentrated on her walking and looked at the scenery. She interrupted him at intervals to ask what certain birds were called, the answer to which he did not know, or the names of certain trees, to which he answered vaguely. She noticed he had begun to be short of breath as they walked and hoped that soon he would have had enough exercise and return home. But of course he did not. He did stop talking, though, concentrating on his breathing. As they walked round a bend in the lane, two figures were coming towards them. One was Polly, the other her master. Polly remembered Christie and wagged her tail.

'Hello, Polly, you remember me?' Christie gave her a pat. 'Good morning, Mr Allard.' Then she introduced the two men. Martin Allard's eyes wandered from one to the other and summed up the situation immediately.

'And how do you like it in the south of England, Mr Bush?' he asked.

'I only came yesterday, so I have come to no conclusion as yet. I hope to like it, as I shall be taking over Mrs Ford's house. My Mother, you see, will return to Yorkshire and my Father.'

'And what does your father do?'

'We are in the textile industry. We hope to expand the trade by employing the home spinners and weavers as out-workers. I am down here to visit Bristol and to do the buying part of our enterprise. When I live here it will be so much easier, especially seeing the quality of the cotton at first hand.' He puffed out his chest a little as he said this.

Martin, wishing to liven up this conversation, said: 'Ah! Miss Farrell will be able to tell you about cotton. She's an expert.'

Milton looked surprised. 'Really?'

'No, not really,' said Christie, looking indignantly at Martin. 'My Father owns a cotton plantation, that is all.'

'And do you have slaves like the one you brought with you?' asked Milton.

'No we do not. We have workers. And many of them, like Zilpah, have been offered their freedom, which they have turned down because they like working and being with us.'

Christie looked annoyed and Milton surprised but Martin just grinned. He changed the subject by saying: 'Miss Farrell, you are looking much better, you know. When I saw you last I would have called you little Miss Winter with your pale face and pink nose.' Here he touched it lightly with the tip of a finger and as she looked quickly up at him she saw the laughter in his hazel eyes. He went on:

'In Celia's face a question did arise
Which were more beautiful, her lips or eyes?'

'And what was the answer, sir?' asked Christie, smiling at him.

'I'll tell you tonight, when you come to Mrs Henshaw's dinner.' As she looked startled he went on: 'You *do* remember, don't you?'

Christie understood. 'Yes, yes, of course I remember. Thank you.'

'Bring Zilpah with you. I'll send the carriage.'

'Thank you.'

He said 'good day', raised his hat and called to Polly. Then he went on his way, a broad grin on his face.

'Odd fellow,' sniffed Milton. 'Quotes poetry.'

Christie did not answer; her mind was elsewhere. How did Mr Allard know how she felt? Did it show so badly? And why did he particularly mention Zilpah? Was it to show that she was to be chaperoned? Oh, well, she would probably find out this evening. She smiled. Mr Allard's company would be preferable to the Bushes' any time. She must buy some flowers to take to Mrs Henshaw.

Abruptly she turned. 'Let us go back,' she said.

Thankfully Milton obeyed.

Chapter 16

The carriage came at the appointed time and Christie, wearing a dress the colour of mulberries with a quilted underskirt and falls of cream lace at her elbows, was surprised to see Zilpah in what she called 'her dress for special occasions.'

'Why, Zilpah, you look very nice,' remarked Christie, raising her eyebrows.

'So do you, Miss Christie.'

Christie said no more but wondered what was going on. 'You know,' she said, 'we must shop for more clothes for you, Zilpah. I'm sure you could do with some, especially dresses.'

Zilpah surprised her yet again by saying: 'Dat would be nice.' Usually she disclaimed and said she would not know what to do with too many.

They finished their short journey in silence, each immersed in their own thoughts. When they arrived Christie walked to the front door of the Manor, it being held open in readiness by Perkins, and Zilpah continued in the carriage, which conveyed her to the servants' quarters.

Christie was shown into a small room where Martin Allard and his aunt were waiting. After the usual greetings Christie presented Mrs Henshaw with a large bunch of narcissi. Her face wreathed in smiles, she said, 'Oh, thank you. I do so like flowers and these always make me think that spring is on its way. You must stay at least until the spring, it is so lovely here then.'

Christie smiled, not knowing what else to reply.

Then they sat and chatted about the weather and the state of the roads and Mrs Henshaw said she was pleased to see Christie again, although Christie had the feeling that she had not remembered her at all. Then dinner was announced and Martin, with a lady on each arm, entered the dining room.

Over the very pleasant meal of tomato and carrot soup, baked mutton with caper sauce, stewed pheasants with chestnuts and vegetable dishes such as buttered parsnips and turnips with an orange sauce, followed by syllabubs and fruit pies, they talked on various topical subjects. Then Martin asked Christie what her plans were.

'Well, as far as I know at the moment I shall move to a house of my own as soon as possible. I was wondering, though, while I was waiting, if I could travel a little. It might be the time to do it as I am not too happy with Mrs Bush and it would be easier for us all if I removed myself.'

'Where did you think of going?'

'Not too far, especially in this cold weather. Perhaps it might be a good idea to visit Bristol or Bath. Which would you suggest is the better place?'

Mrs Henshaw said she would much prefer Bath at this time of year. 'There is the theatre, you know, and the dances. But do not drink the waters, dear, they taste horrid.' They laughed.

Eventually dinner was over and as they moved to the withdrawing room, Mrs Henshaw, without worrying about leaving them on their own, said she would retire and have an early night, if they didn't mind. Martin looked a little startled but opened the door for his Aunt.

'I'm sorry,' he said to Christie, 'she forgets. Do you mind being alone with me? I'm serious,' he added as Christie grinned.

'No, of course not. Polly is here. I'm sure she will protect me from harm, won't you, Polly?' Polly, hearing her name, managed to lift her head, took one look, wagged a weary tail and went back to sleep. 'See?' laughed Christie. 'Besides, you have been so kind to me I feel as if I know you quite well. The dinner was delicious, by the way. It was kind of you to invite me at such short notice.'

'Well, I could see the problem. Mr Bush is a most boring young man, I should think.'

Christie thought she had better change the subject. 'Tell me about Langley Manor, Mr Allard. It looks a very interesting building.'

'Shall we dispense with surnames?'

'Very well, Martin.'

'I will show you round when you come over in daylight, and perhaps I could show you the garden. I haven't been here long, you know. It's not handed down in the family. I came from London after my parents died. This house was for sale, so I bought it and I enjoy it very much and the surroundings. London was never to my taste. I prefer the country. Do you ride, Christie? What a silly question.

With your background I am sure you do.' Christie nodded. 'Good. When the weather is better, we will ride. I have horses in the stables, other than the carriage horses, so I am sure there will be one suitable for you.'

'And what do you do apart from ride?' asked Christie.

'Do you think I am a frippery fellow with nothing to do?' He laughed at her.

Christie blushed. 'I'm sorry, I didn't mean to sound rude.'

'You didn't. Well, I am responsible for the cultivation of my land and the wellbeing of my tenants. I'm involved with village problems and I'm a magistrate of the area. When I have time, I indulge myself with some fishing or ornithology. I don't hunt, though, and I don't shoot unless in a duel or something.'

'A duel? Have you ever shot anyone—or shouldn't I ask?' said Christie, round eyed.

'I haven't killed anyone, if that's what you mean, but I have winged one or two people over the years.'

'Gracious.'

Martin smiled. 'Don't worry, I'm harmless really.'

'I saw some birds this morning when I was with Milton Bush. I asked him what they were and, do you know he could not tell me? I would have thought he would know some of them at least.'

'What an ignorant fellow he is, to be sure,' said Martin with a twinkle in his eye. 'And what are the birds called in Charleston, dare one ask?'

With a prim face Christie said: 'One dare. Near us, as we're close to the Ashley river, we have wood stork, ibis, egrets, white tails and bald eagles. We also have the smaller birds like the wren, thrasher and the cardinal but I think he comes from further north.'

'They all sound very different to ours. I must go some day and find out for myself.'

'You would be made very welcome.'

'Thank you,' he said seriously.

Changing the subject, Christie asked: 'Martin, why did you say I was to bring Zilpah with me particularly this evening? And why has she put on her best dress, do you think?'

'Well, we were talking in front of Mr Bush, weren't we? It was best to mention bringing a servant with you. I could just see him telling tales to his Mama.'

Christie frowned at him. 'You're teasing me, I think.'

'I don't tell secrets,' was all he said.

After that, Christie thought it time to leave.

Martin pulled the bell cord and ordered the carriage to take Christie home. In the hall, Perkins held her cloak. She thanked Martin again for inviting her, smiling at him as her fingers fumbled trying to fasten her cloak.

'Ah, I forgot,' he said, removing her fingers and performing the task for her. 'I said I would finish the poem for you, didn't I?'

'Yes,' said Christie. 'I thought you must have forgotten it,' she laughed.

With a twinkle in his eyes and fingers still holding her by her cloak, he recited:

> *'In Celia's face a question did arise*
> *Which were more beautiful, her lips or eyes.*
> *"We," said the eyes, "send forth those pointed darts*
> *Which pierce the hardest adamantine hearts."*
> *"From us," replied the lips, "proceed those blisses*
> *Which lovers reap by kind words and kisses."'*

As he finished, he kissed her lightly on the lips. He said softly, 'Goodnight, Christie,' and turned.

Christie stood in shock for a moment, then, pulling herself together, hurried out of the door, which was held open by the footman who, his demeanour aloof as usual, pretended not to have noticed anything untoward.

Meanwhile, Martin went to his library, his inner sanctum, where he could think and relax. He poured himself a glass of wine. Was he serious about Christie or had he only dalliance in mind? That was fun and agreeable, but if that's all it was he should stop now. Christie was in a very vulnerable state. She had been deeply unhappy—that was why she came to England, so that she could get away from something or someone. He was pleased to think he had helped her recover a little, but did he really want to know her further? Marriage was a big step. Did he want to take it that far? Blowed if he knew, but she was the first one he had thought about in this way, so it must mean something positive—that, or he was getting bored with his own company. He frowned. Well, he would just see how things progressed. Perhaps Christie would indicate how she felt sometime. She was certainly interesting to know and came from a good family who seemed well educated and one who had money. But the monetary side was no problem—he had plenty of his own. He would just have to wait and see how things evolved. Something would decide him one way or another.

He felt too unsettled to retire, so decided to write a short note to his cousin and a long overdue letter to his brother. After this, no doubt, he would be tired enough to sleep.

The next two days Christie busied herself by taking Zilpah and Mary shopping, mainly to choose material for Zilpah's new dresses. She liked bright colours, so Christie enjoyed watching her choose. She also liked to have a bandana on her head so material for these were chosen too. Christie thought it unfair that Mary should accompany them, give them the benefit of her knowledge of materials and patterns and not have something new herself. So Mary had material for a new dress, too, much to her delight. Christie asked for them to be made by the seamstress at the shop, so all the ladies had to do was wait until the dresses could be delivered.

The following day Christie was thrilled to receive three letters. She had stepped into the hall to take them from the carrier and pay him when Mrs Bush saw her. 'Miss Farrell, would you give me a few moments of your time, if it's convenient?' she asked.

Surprised at the tone, Christie just said, 'Yes, of course.' When they had sat down in the morning room Mrs Bush frowned a little and then said: 'Miss Farrell, I wish to say something and it is a delicate subject. So please be patient with me.'

'Of course,' said Christie, again wondering what was coming and why Mrs Bush was being so polite and nice.

'I want to speak to you about Milton. He is a hard working boy and very intelligent although I shouldn't say so, of course. I believe he will go far in the business. I think he has told you he is to live here. I know you are thinking of moving but as the house is so big there is no need, you know.'

Christie began to frown. What was she about to hear? She began to feel uncomfortable. Mrs Bush continued: 'No, no need at all. You see, he does like you a lot and forgive me for saying this, but with that mark on your face, you won't have much chance of marriage elsewhere, will you? So I thought it would be a good idea to...'

She got no further. 'No!' shouted Christie, making Mrs Bush jump. 'No, no, no! How dare you propose such a thing? If Mr Bush wants to marry me, he should ask me himself. But the answer would still be the same. No, no, no.' She stood up and marched out, then ran up the stairs to her own room. How dare that woman speak to her like that? She stood by the window, seething. What a horrid person Mrs Bush was! How dare she suggest such a thing? The sooner she moved house the better. She wouldn't stay here a minute longer. It may be true that no one would want to marry her, but it was unkind in Mrs Bush to say so. She dashed away the tears. She would *not* let that woman upset her.

She took some deep breaths, concentrating on the view from her window, then she suddenly remembered her letters. A watery smile lit up her face as she saw one was from home with Papa's writing on the envelope. A lovely fat letter it was, too. But the others? She opened one that was perfumed. It was quite short and from a Mrs James in Bath inviting her to stay for a few days so that she could see the delights of the city. Christie was to let her know when it was convenient for her to visit. Now, who was Mrs James, and how did she know Christie wished to go there? She thought hard. The only person she had discussed it with was Martin. Did he know this Mrs James? Was this his doing? Oh, dear! Since dining at the Manor she had tried not to think of what had happened. Was Martin just having fun at her expense? Surely he wasn't the kind of person to do that, but she dare not let herself think otherwise. But she must find out who Mrs James was so she would have to see him soon. She felt pleasure in the fact but pushed the feeling away and hurriedly ripped open the third letter. It was a short note from Mr Wicks saying he would call that afternoon and take her to view a house on the outskirts of Stanton and hoped the time would be convenient. Oh, thank goodness for that! To remove herself from the Bush household at last! Gracious, everything was happening at once. She must see Zilpah and tell her to be ready to accompany her. But first she must read the letter from home.

My dear Christie (wrote Papa)

It was good to receive your letter and to know you had both arrived safely but I was saddened to learn that my cousin had died. How are you managing? I am sure though, that you will be all right with Zilpah to look after you. Tell her that Jacob is well and happy and sends his love. We all miss you but hope you are feeling better and enjoying England. Also, that you have made new friends.

You will be pleased, I know, to hear that the Winthrops are moving away soon and that their workers are much happier since I am keeping an eye on them. I must finish now as the girls are writing to you separately.

Grandmama sends you much love, as do we all.

Write when you can

Yours affectionately

Papa

The letters from Christie's sisters were about their social activities and entertainments, the young men they had met and a description of their new dresses. Carrie particularly wanted to know what the young men were like in England, was it cold and what was the food like? They all sent their love to her and Zilpah.

By the time Christie had finished reading she felt much better, albeit a little homesick. She pushed that to one side and went to find Zilpah to give her the message about Jacob and to ask her to be ready to accompany her that afternoon to go with Mr Wicks to see the house where they were to live.

Chapter 17

The house was situated at the other end of the village to that of the late Mrs Ford. Christie thought the further away she was from Mrs Bush the better. From the outside she saw two windows on either side of a central door, and basement windows below. The house was the end one of three. To Christie's eyes it looked quite small, but inside, when she had trod up the three steps and entered, she was pleasantly surprised. The rooms were not large but they were adequate and from the look of it had been freshly cleaned and polished. The dining room led off the entrance hall and the withdrawing room, which was the largest room, was on the next floor. It was all tastefully decorated and the furniture of a reasonably good quality. She visited the bedrooms and then went down to the basement to see the kitchen.

'Well, Zilpah, what do you think?'

Zilpah nodded. 'I t'ink it nice house. It feel good.'

So when Christie had seen and inspected everything she went to see Mr Wicks who was waiting for her in the dining room.

'Shall we discuss this?' he asked with a smile. 'What do you think?'

'I think it will do very well if I can afford it.'

'It is rented, of course, and the price is reasonable, I think.' He named the figure and Christie was surprised.

'I would have expected to pay more,' she said.

'The staff come in each day. They live in the village, you know. They come in early and leave late so there should be no inconvenience. It seems to work well. But you can have them stay overnight if you so wish.'

'When can I move in?' asked Christie.

'Any time. Tomorrow, if that is convenient. I can have everything and everyone assembled ready.'

'Then tomorrow it is,' said Christie with a smile. As an afterthought she said: 'I shall need use of a carriage. Where can I find someone?'

'Ah,' Mr Wicks said. 'There is no room here for your own, I'm afraid, but if you let Len Woods know, he's not far away; he will drive you anywhere you wish to go at any time. He's a reliable fellow and will be pleased of the work.'

'Who are my neighbours? I shall have to make myself known to them.'

'They are very nice people. Next door is Mr Franks. He's a retired naval man. Quiet, I should think. The other house is occupied by a Mrs Hayes and her four children.'

'No Mr Hayes?' Mr Wicks shook his head.

Christie wondered if there was a problem here but she asked no more questions, as she was sure Mr Wicks would not gossip. So she just nodded.

Everything was settled to Christie's satisfaction. They left the house and said goodbye to Mr Wicks and went in search of Len Woods. Christie found him just a short way from the village. He was an elderly rotund man with a round face to match topped by a balding head surrounded by a fringe of white hair. She asked if he could be ready to move them the following morning.

'I'll be there, ma'am, with me carriage all right and tight, ma'am,' said Len with a cheery grin.

Then Christie and Zilpah hurried back to appraise the Bushes of their departure on the morrow. Also, Christie told Mary to be packed and ready to leave after breakfast.

The following day all went according to plan, even Milton seeing them off with a smile. Christie thought he was pleased to see her go, so that he could establish his own authority in the running of the house. His mother, after being informed of Christie leaving the previous day, kept out of the way, much to Christie's relief. She had said her goodbyes to Mrs Cardew and the staff the previous evening and thanked them for their support when she had first arrived. It was funny, she mused, as she sat in the carriage for the short journey to her own house, how she had hoped, when she had first come, for Mrs Ford to be a mother figure and a comfort to her. As it was, she had had to fight through everything for herself with no one to help her. Of course, that was not strictly true—there was always dear Zilpah and, surprisingly, Martin Allard. Perhaps that was what she had wanted, though—someone to show her how to overcome her difficulties and get on with life.

She didn't have time to think any more as they were now outside the house and Mr Wicks was there ready and waiting. The two girls from the village looked pleasant enough with their scrubbed faces smiling at her. One was Mattie, the other Peggy.

Bags and baggage were carried to the appropriate rooms and after a reasonable time for everyone to settle in, Christie called for a meeting of all to attend so that duties could be established. Mattie and Peggy did what they usually did which was to keep the house clean and any other jobs that they were asked to do. Zilpah would cook and generally supervise everything in the kitchen as she used to at home in Charleston, which left Mary to organise Christie's personal requirements. Christie came to the conclusion she must be the bookkeeper. She had some idea about this work watching Mr Pope at home poring over her father's ledgers, but she had never been shown properly 'how to keep the books'. She would learn, though, she told herself.

Now, a walk to the shops would be a gentle exercise and some fresh air invigorating, so accompanied by Mary, it wasn't long before she was the possessor of a thick ledger. Christie, realising Saint Peter's church was nearer now, decided to have another look round the interior. She sent Mary back home with the ledger and walked the few steps down the lane to where the church stood. When the weather was a little warmer, she decided she would look at the gargoyles outside and the gravestones, some of which were decidedly old. But at the moment, as the wind was whipping round the church, it was much more comfortable to be inside. As on her previous visit, the interior was sombre with a damp air and she wished some candles could have been lit, but she managed to read some of the plaques, which were commemorations of previous inhabitants of Stanton and she noticed one, which mentioned "he was of the Manor". She was going nearer to have a closer look when a voice said: 'Good afternoon, Miss Farrell.'

She turned to find a young man smiling at her. He continued: 'I'm Lucius Thripp, the vicar here.' He was tall and fair-haired with a thin face. He stooped slightly.

Christie smiled at him. 'How nice to meet you, Mr Thripp. How did you know my name?'

'This is a village, although a large one. Nothing is secret, you know. Was there something you wished to see particularly? Shall I light a candle for you to see better?'

'No, no. I have been in before but I thought I'd take another look at some of the things I missed then.'

'You are welcome to come any time. Perhaps you would like to join us on Sunday at our morning service? You would be most welcome.'

'Thank you. I would have come before, but…'

'You have been ill,' Mr Thripp finished for her. 'I know these things, you see.'

Christie smiled ruefully. 'Oh dear, I shall have to be careful in future, won't I?'

Mr Thripp smiled back. 'Would you like me to give you some information about the church?'

'Thank you.'

Half an hour later Christie left, pleased to have met the vicar, a pleasant young man, she thought, and to learn a little more about Stanton. She made a mental note also to attend church the next Sunday morning.

When she arrived home a surprise awaited her. Martin had called and Zilpah had shown him into the withdrawing room.

'Martin, I'm so sorry. Have you been here long?'

'No, Christie. I thought I would call and see how you are settling in, that is all.'

'Thank you, how kind. I think we are all right. We have only been here since this morning, so it is quite new to us all. How did you know I had moved?'

'In a village…' he began, spreading his fingers.

'I know, "nothing is secret", to quote the vicar's words.'

'Ah! Is that where you were, talking to our Lucius?'

'Yes, he is very kind, isn't he? Is there a Mrs Thripp?'

'Not as I know of. Why, are you enamoured of him after the first meeting?' Martin looked at her, a mischievous smile hovering on his lips.

'Certainly not.' She frowned at him. 'But the village hasn't passed on the information to me yet,' she said a shade waspishly. He laughed out loud. 'Touché,' he said. 'Oh, I forgot, Zilpah said she'd bring tea.'

'Oh, yes,' said Christie, turning the tables. 'You have made a conquest there, you know.'

'I know,' he said, surprising her. 'My conquests are all over the place.'

'Have you no shame, sir?' asked Christie.

'Not really,' was the laughing reply.

'Which reminds me. I've had a letter from a Mrs Sally James, kindly asking me to visit her in Bath. Now I wondered if you had anything to do with this, as she doesn't say how she knows me and I'm sure the Stanton village gossip doesn't reach Bath. You are the only one I've mentioned it to, so am I right in assuming you know her?'

'That's right. I do. She should have mentioned the fact when she wrote to you but she is a bit of a scatterbrain. Will you go? I'm sure you'd like her.'

'I think so, perhaps next week if it is convenient for her. She is very kind to invite me since she hasn't even met me.'

'Let me know when it is arranged and I will send Toby and the carriage for you.'

'Oh, thank you but…'

Zilpah interrupted by bringing in the tea so Christie sat and concentrated on pouring the golden liquid into the delicate china bowls.

'Did you pour the tea when you were at home?' asked Martin, changing the subject.

'Sometimes, when I was there. Emma usually did that kind of thing. I was usually busy looking after the younger ones or Papa. Then there was the staff to keep happy and the workers. I was very busy.'

'No gentleman friends to take you out away from it all?'

A stricken look passed over Christie's face. She looked down at her hands. 'No, no, nothing like that,' she whispered.

Martin looked at her. He had evidently touched a vulnerable spot. Was it something to do with that scar?

'Well,' went on Martin as if he hadn't noticed anything different. 'Is there anything else that worries you that I can help you with?'

Christie smiled quickly. 'Thank you, but no…' Then a thought occurred to her. 'Unless you know something about bookkeeping?'

Martin laughed. 'What do you wish to know?'

Christie showed him the ledger.

'Come and sit by me, then,' he said, 'and I'll show you what you must do.'

Chapter 18

The following morning Christie had a stream of callers. Mary had warned her that this could happen, as short morning calls were the custom. If longer calls were needed, arrangements were made to meet at a later date or invitations given. Mary also pointed out that a young lady should have a chaperone at all times, even if only a maid. This problem was solved by Mary being present, or if she was absent for any reason, Zilpah. Zilpah was far happier in her own domain in the kitchen but she said that 'If Miss Christie needed her, she would be dere.'

Christie was pleased it wasn't Zilpah who answered the door when her first caller came that morning. She was surprised to see Milton walk into the room. At first she did not recognise him as he was wearing a wig. Now Christie, like everyone else, was used to gentlemen and ladies wearing wigs. Her father wore one at home sometimes for formal occasions, but somehow in Stanton at this time of day the type of wig Milton was wearing seemed very much out of place. It was a tie-wig, brushed up high in the front away from the face and looking wonderful on a man with classical features, but Milton, unfortunately, was not blessed with these and it just emphasised his round baby face all the more. It did give him height, though, which was probably why he had chosen it. Christie wanted to laugh but kept her face straight as she curtseyed.

'Good morning, Milton, how kind of you to call.'

'I thought I should,' he said as he tried to sit elegantly on a chair but with his short figure failed miserably. 'After all,' he went on, 'you are alone here and I didn't wish you to be unhappy. The house is rather small, though, isn't it? You could have stayed in mine, you know. My Mother is there, so there would have been no problems.'

Christie thought that there would have been plenty of problems but did not say so. She replied instead: 'Thank you, but I think it best this way. Would you like a glass of wine?'

'Thank you. There is something special I wish to say to you.'

'Is there?'

Before this conversation could be carried further, however, the doorknocker sounded and Lucius Thripp was shown in. Milton looked a little put out but Christie was relieved. The vicar was much easier to talk to. He said he was pleased to meet Milton at last and asked if he would like to attend the service on Sunday. Milton nodded after giving it some thought.

'If Miss Farrell intends to be there, then I shall too,' said Milton seriously. Christie could have cheerfully hit him. He then took his leave saying he would call again but in the meantime begging Christie to contact him if she was worried about anything.

Christie said nothing but managed to smile goodbye, but inside she was seething. He was the last person she would go to for help and why did he have to be so patronising? She was just going to make a remark to Mr Thripp when there was a knock on the door and Christie looked up hopefully. But a young lady came in. 'Good morning,' she said. 'Do you remember me, Miss Farrell? We met at Mr Allard's. At the Manor, I mean. I am Ann Smythe. Oh, good morning, Mr Thripp,' she finished, seeing Lucius standing there smiling at her. She blushed as she curtseyed.

'How nice of you to call,' Christie said. She remembered the girl; she had been the quietest in the group. She was pretty with soft brown hair and dark eyes. Evidently she knew the vicar quite well and it was pleasant to have an easier conversation now Milton had left. Then Lucius decided to take his leave. He thanked Christie for her hospitality, said he hoped to see Ann and her mama soon, which made Ann blush even more.

As the door closed Ann said, 'I thought I must come and apologise for our behaviour to you when we were at the Manor. We were very unkind and I'm sorry.' Her brown eyes looked anxiously at Christie.

'Thank you,' said Christie, 'but I believe you were not to blame. I don't think you said anything you should not have said.'

'That's just it,' said Ann. 'I didn't like what Frances said to you but I didn't stand up and say so. I just went and sat with her when I should have stayed with you. It was cowardly of me. It has worried me ever since, so I thought now you are on your own in your own home, I must make the effort to come and tell you that I'm sorry.'

Christie smiled. 'Thank you, that is very kind of you. Let us forget all about it, shall we? You are welcome to visit me whenever you like.'

'Oh, yes, and you must visit me too. I will give you my direction before I leave. Mama, too, will be pleased to meet you but she thinks it unusual for a young lady to set up house on her own. I told her that I believed some people in the Americas do this, so she understood.' Christie smiled at this but said nothing. 'Of course,' Ann went on, 'the other girls like to go to Langley Manor to see Mr Allard. He is very nice but I find him a little frightening. I prefer Mr Thripp. He is so kind, isn't he?'

'Yes, very,' smiled Christie.

'Well,' said Ann standing up, 'Here is my card. I must go now as Mama will worry although I did bring my maid with me—but Mothers are like that, aren't they?'

'I suppose they are,' agreed Christie.

She was pleased that her first morning had gone well. One person had been missing, though, which would have made the morning complete, she thought wistfully, but as he had visited the previous afternoon she could not expect it. Obviously as he had lived at Langley Manor for some time, he took the duties that went with it seriously and watched everyone's welfare, if possible. So his calling yesterday was probably a routine visit, as far as he was concerned. Christie gave a sigh.

Chapter 19

The gossips in Stanton were having a wonderful time. Not as far back as they could remember had they been so diverted. Mrs Brewer, the grandam of the busybody society and the hub of the tittle-tattlers, was in great form. She held forth to her bosom friends, who, in their turn, told their tales of up to date 'goings on' in the village.

So it was that the visitors to Christie's house were the main topic on the following morning. 'And did you see,' said Mrs Brewer, 'that young man who came from Yorkshire, the one who is to live in old Mrs Ford's house, visit Miss Farrell? Milton's his name. Did you ever hear such a name? And did you ever see such a sight as when he strutted along wearing that wig?' Here she tried to give an impression of what Milton had looked like, but as she was a large lady with an ample bosom, the picture of him was lost. However, she went on: 'Then the vicar called. I wonder if he rates his chances high in the marriage stakes. But they do say that Miss Farrell is wealthy, so perhaps he's hoping for a fat donation to the church instead. Then Mr Allard visits her, but not yesterday. He visits everyone, though, doesn't he?' She sniffed. 'But you never know, we must keep an eye open.' She nodded wisely and the hangers-on nodded their heads too.

'I wonder how Miss Farrell came by that scar on her face? Someone said she was whipped,' said one of the gossips.

'I don't really know the answer to that one yet,' said Mrs Brewer. 'But I shall eventually. Of course, these foreigners do funny things, don't they?' She nodded again. Her followers nodded too. Mrs Brewer knew these things.

They all reported their own pieces of gossip from around the village to Mrs Brewer, then departed to spread her words further.

Had Christie known her affairs were looked upon with so much interest she would have been amused. To think she was so important to warrant this would never have entered her head. Mr Allard's affairs, though, must always be of interest to everyone as he had lived at Langley Manor for some time and was a local magistrate, to boot. Christie was seeing him in this light now, as she had learnt when talking to people, that he was kind and helpful to everyone, especially those in trouble. Well, he certainly had been kind to her but she must not take it too personally and, of course, he liked his fun—but she was sure nothing more was intended. 'How could it possibly be,' she thought, looking in the mirror as she did every night when she rubbed in Mrs Larkin's special cream. She thought it was helping to soften the skin and the puckering of the scar was not quite so tight, which was wonderful. But Mrs Bush was right, no one would really want to marry her and look at a face like that every day. How could she expect it? She didn't. 'What you will do, my girl,' she told herself severely, 'is to enjoy yourself and forget about the scar and marriage.' After all, she would probably return back home soon anyway. There was plenty to keep her occupied there. But she found, if she was really honest, she did not wish to return yet. She was happy in her little house, something Papa and the girls would not understand, she thought, and she was just beginning to feel that she now belonged to Stanton in a small way. She felt she must stay a little longer at all events.

Her thoughts were interrupted by the doorknocker sounding. She heard Zilpah answer it but as no one came in she did not bother to move. Zilpah was talking and laughing, then eventually shut the door.

'Who was that?' Christie called.

'I's coming, Miss Christie,' said Zilpah, appearing in the doorway. 'It a note from Mis' Allard.'

'Oh? Who were you talking to, then?'

'Jest the man who bring it.'

Christie looked at Zilpah. She seemed very pleased with herself. What was going on?

The note was brief.

Christie.
Unless you let me know otherwise, we will ride this afternoon.
I will call about 2 o'clock.
            Martin

'Did the messenger wait?'

'No. D'you want to send message, den?'

'Mm, not really. Mr Allard says we will ride this afternoon. Could you press my habit for me, Zilpah, please? I hung it up, but…'

'Don't worry. I see it nice.'

'Thank you, Zilpah. I shall just have time to pay a quick call on my neighbours before lunch. I shan't need much to eat, Zilpah, if I'm riding.'

'Huh,' was the reply.

She knocked on Mr Franks' door first. It was answered by a middle-aged servant who looked as though he had been in the navy, if his weather-beaten face and the tattoos on his bare arms were anything to go by. She was asked inside and eventually shown into a room full of naval memorabilia in the centre of which sat Mr Franks in a comfortable armchair. His fresh complexion and white beard, as well as the naval jacket, gave him a distinguished look. He evidently found rising difficult without help, so Christie hurriedly broke in: 'Please do not bother to rise, sir. I have only come for a few minutes to introduce myself. I'm Christie Farrell and I am your new neighbour.'

'Oh? Kind of you to call. Sit there.' He pointed to a chair. 'A drink?' He pointed to a decanter.

'No, thank you,' Christie said hurriedly, eyeing the dark golden liquid which looked like rum. 'I cannot stay long this time as I have Mrs Hayes to see, too. But I will visit you again if you would like me to.' She smiled at him.

'Very nice,' he said in his abrupt way. 'I'd like you to. Do you play chess?'

'Ye-es, but not very well, I fear.'

'Don't matter,' said Mr Franks, his face brightening. 'Like to see you again.'

'Thank you. I shall certainly come, sir, if I may.'

Mrs Hayes' house was completely different insofar as it was much noisier. A girl of about ten years old opened the door to Christie. She could hear other children arguing and crying. Christie said: 'Is your Mama in? My name is Christie Farrell and I've just come to live near you.'

'My name is Beth Hayes. Please come in.'

Christie was surprised the girl was so cool and calm with the noise going on in the background. Her clothes were of poor quality but clean as were her face and hands. Christie was shown into a room, which looked as though it was kept just for visitors. It was clean and the furniture polished. Beth asked her to sit down while she fetched her mother. In a few minutes Mrs Hayes came and the children's shouts stopped. No doubt they had been told a visitor had arrived. Mrs

Hayes looked tired and worn with a thin pointed face. She probably looked older than her years. 'I beg your pardon for coming at a difficult time,' Christie began.

'Please sit down. It doesn't matter. The little ones will settle eventually.'

'How old are they?'

'Beth is ten, Chloe eight, then John is six and Phoebe five.'

'It must be difficult to keep them occupied all the time.'

'Some days are better than others. Sometimes they go and see a lady in the village. She gives them lessons and then I have time to clean for Mr Franks.'

'I see. Well, this is a quick call, so I won't keep you. But could I see the children before I go? Where are they?'

'Oh, Miss Farrell, they are in the kitchen and it's ever so untidy.'

'That's to be expected with four children,' smiled Christie. 'Don't worry, I'm the eldest of four children and I remember the messes we got into.'

For the first time Mrs Hayes smiled, which lightened up her face making her look quite pretty. 'Well, come along if you are sure.'

Beth was in charge of the children where they were occupied with their toys, such as they were. Little Phoebe was getting soaked, by pouring water into pots. She was concentrating hard so as not to spill. The others played with toys that had seen better days and the use of their imaginations was essential.

'Hello children,' Christie said quietly. Hearing her accent they all looked up quickly. 'You all look very busy.'

After one look at her they all decided to tell her what they were doing and it was noisy once again. Eventually, Christie said: 'Thank you all for telling me. I have to go now but perhaps your Mama will let you visit me. I must tell you I have a black lady living with me so you must come and meet her too.'

This last piece of information quietened them.

'When can I come?' asked John. 'I want to see the black lady.'

'I will let you know,' said Christie.

As Christie left, Mrs Hayes thanked her for coming. She must do something to help this family, Christie thought. Perhaps she could look after the children occasionally to let their mother have some time to herself. Also she must tell Zilpah that a little boy wanted to meet her.

Christie was ready before two o'clock looking very attractive in a dark blue, severely cut riding habit with a hat to match. She felt nervous, not about riding—she had ridden since she was small—but about seeing Martin again. She frowned but she had no time to worry further as the knocker sounded and Christie answered to find Martin holding the reins of two horses. One was black, the other tan. He smiled at her. 'You look very smart. You should wear that colour more. It suits you.'

'Thank you, kind sir,' was all that Christie said. Then, seeing the horses, she exclaimed, 'Oh, how beautiful!' She went to their heads and stroked them.

'This one is yours,' said Martin, indicating the tan mare.

'She's lovely. What's her name?'

'Cherry. I'm pleased you like her.'

Christie spent a little while petting both horses and giving them carrots. Martin waited patiently for her to finish and then said simply: 'Shall we go?'

Christie hardly needed Martin's help to climb into the saddle, as she was so agile.

'I thought we would ride outside on to the hills where there are some good gallops and views. Then back to the Manor, all right?'

'That sounds wonderful. I haven't ridden for some time so this is a great treat.'

'We must do it more often then, when the weather is fine. You are welcome to come and take Cherry out any time, but you must be accompanied by someone other than myself if I'm not available.'

'Pooh,' said Christie, having ridden alone at home many times. Then seeing the set of his lips went on: 'Thank you for the offer. I love to ride.'

'But you must promise to have someone with you when you do,' he insisted, and looked straight at her.

'Oh, all right, I promise. But I used to go on my own at home.'

'Maybe, but as I am responsible for you when you ride my horse...'

'I have promised, Martin.'

He nodded. They spent the next two hours galloping, trotting and walking the horses, also stopping to admire the scenery. Martin and Christie were pleased with each other as both rode well and so they enjoyed themselves. When it was time to return to the Manor, Christie felt pleasantly tired. It was easy to tell she had enjoyed herself as her cheeks were flushed and her eyes sparkled.

'Thank you, Martin, I really enjoyed it,' she said as she gave Cherry a final pat and handed her over to the groom.

'So did I,' he said with a smile. He led the way to the library where he poured out glasses of wine for them both. A dish of sweetmeats had been placed on the table.

'My Aunt is probably still in her room. I hope you don't mind,' said Martin.

'I don't mind your Aunt being in her room,' grinned Christie.

'You know what I mean, so be serious.'

'Sorry, yes, Martin, and I don't mind, Martin. Oh look, here comes Polly. She evidently knows I have need of her.'

Polly had pushed open the door when she had heard Martin come in, went to them both for a pat, and settled herself before the fire after being fussed over.

'You've become very cheeky since I first met you,' said Martin, sitting down.

'That is because I am much better and I'm my usual self again. I believe I have you to thank for much of that, though,' Christie said seriously.

'It is just a matter of getting through illness and the problems that go with it, that's all. I'm pleased you are recovered.'

Then Christie told Martin of her visitors and about Milton's wig. 'I think he feels that now he is in possession of his own house he sees himself as a figure to be looked up to. Who would do that I don't really know because he looked a real buffle.' She giggled.

'A what?' asked Martin, stiffening.

'Did I not hear that word properly then?' asked Christie primly.

'No. If you mean a fool, say so. Don't revert to words you've picked up and don't know what they mean. You'll find yourself in trouble.'

'Like now?' asked Christie.

Martin's face softened. 'No, of course not.'

'Tell me about the Manor then, please.'

'Come, I'll show you.'

The Manor was larger than Christie realised. Parts of it, like the porch, dated back to the fifteenth century. It also had panelled rooms including the library. The staircase was of a later date, in the seventeenth century. There were a few portraits of Martin's ancestors but mainly the oil paintings were of scenes, horses and dogs. Some of the smaller rooms were unused but Martin told Christie he would gradually have them furnished so that they could be. At the moment he and his aunt only occupied the main rooms. Christie admired it all and asked questions and told Martin how different it all was to where she lived. She loved the mellow stonework outside so Martin suggested that, if she were not too tired, they take a walk in the garden as there was something he would like to show her.

The garden at the back of the house stretched for some distance and looked pleasant but would be more so when spring arrived bringing the flowers. Martin said: 'The helibores are about finished, as you can see, but later we have the papavers, cyclamen and, of course, roses.' There was some lawn, which was left at the moment. No doubt the gardeners would scythe it later in the growing season. They walked on and Christie saw bushes and recognised holly and bay. Martin pointed out the blackbirds to her, the thrushes and sparrows and even a robin came hoping for food.

'Ah, here we are. Do you recognise these, Christie?' He pointed to some tall trees.

Christie looked and opened her eyes wide. 'Why, they look like the poplar trees we have at home,' she began.

'Well done, they are. They are Carolina poplars. I've had them some years now.'

'But—but where did you get them from?'

'Carolina, where else? I had them shipped over.'

'Good gracious! And they grow well here too?' Christie wanted to ask him how and why he had them shipped over but did not like to be inquisitive. So she just said: 'Thank you for showing them to me—and all your garden. I'm sure it will look lovely in the spring too. Seeing the poplars was a little bit of home. Thank you, Martin.'

'You may come again whenever you like.'

'I'd love to. And have you a poem for me today? I haven't heard one lately.'

'Well, let's see,' he said, looking at her consideringly. 'Ah, I know:

> *Robes loosely flowing and aspect as free*
> *A careless carriage decked with modesty.*
> *A smiling look, but yet severe*
> *Such comely graces about her were.'*

Christie laughed. 'I shouldn't have asked, I suppose,' she said 'but I wonder who it was written for originally?' Before he could answer, she went on quickly, 'Thank you for a lovely afternoon, Martin. I really enjoyed it.' She held out her hand.

He took it and held it and said: 'So did I. We must ride again soon. Goodbye, m'dear.' Then he kissed the hand he held before releasing it. 'I'll escort you to the carriage.'

'But I can walk home.'

'You're too tired. Toby will take you.'

Martin said no more, only raised a hand as the carriage moved forward. It wasn't until they arrived home and Zilpah opened the door, her face wreathed in smiles, that Christie realised that Toby was the reason Zilpah looked so pleased with herself. He was a large black man who reminded Christie of Joseph back home.

CHAPTER 20

▼

'And is Toby nice, Zilpah?' asked Christie, later.

'Yes, Miss Christie, he very nice.'

'When did you first meet him then?'

'When we went to Langley Manor, first time. Mis' Allard said I was to go down to Cook and I was to meet Toby. Dat was what Mis' Allard say.'

'I see. Well, if you like him, Zilpah, you can invite him round if you would like to. Perhaps when he has his day off, or…'

'T'ank you,' said Zilpah with a grin. 'Dat would be nice. Oh, I had Cook and little Betsy come round while you were gone, Miss Christie. I took dem into de kitchen for chat and drink. Dat all right?'

'Yes, of course. Why did they come?'

'It was dere af'noon off. Dey had nowhere to go. Dey told me about Mrs Bush.'

'How are they getting on with Mrs Bush and Milton?'

'Dey say that Mrs Bush soon going home, t'ank goodness. De son is stupid but all right. Mrs Cardew manage him well.'

Christie smiled but just nodded.

That night Christie slept well. The fresh air, pleasant company and exercise ensured that she went to bed in a relaxed state of mind conducive to a peaceful sleep. Peaceful, that is, until she was awakened by an urgent shaking. She managed to open her heavy eyes to find Zilpah looking anxiously down on her.

'Miss Christie, Miss Christie. Wake up!'

'What is it, Zilpah? Is someone ill? What time is it?'

'Don't know. Some house on fire. We should help?'

Christie managed to stumble out of bed. 'Where, Zilpah, where?' she began confusedly. Zilpah took her to her room and pointed. Through the window she could see a fire blazing. 'Good gracious.' Christie was awake now. 'Oh, Zilpah, I think it's Mrs Larkin's house. I must go.'

Christie hurried back to her room and managed to put on her shoes, then her heavy winter hood and cloak.

'Miss Christie, you can't go like dat, you wearing only nightgown.'

'My cloak will cover everything. I'll fetch Len, you light a lantern for me.'

'I come,' said Zilpah.

'No, no, you stay here.'

Christie ran down the road in the cold night air, huddled in her cloak. She knocked on Len's door and waited. When he came she told him of the fire and he came out immediately, hurriedly putting on his coat. It didn't take him long to harness the horse to a small open cart. 'It's quicker, ma'am, you see,' he said.

Christie nodded as she climbed up to sit in front with Len. They stopped to collect the lantern from Zilpah on the way and then went as fast as they could bearing in mind the darkness and the rough road. Fortunately, the moon peeped out from behind the clouds from time to time, which helped. When they arrived at the cottage, Christie saw some men already there, taking water from the well and passing it in a variety of containers from hand to hand. One man was on a ladder trying to throw the water over the thatch.

'Where's Mrs Larkin?' shouted Christie.

'She's up at the Manor,' someone answered.

Thank goodness. Christie felt relief sweep over her as she heard the news. She had imagined the worst. Then another thought occurred. 'What about the cat?'

'Don't know,' said a man.

Christie and Len joined the chain of people passing the containers of water, but at the back of Christie's mind was that she must find Tommy. Mrs Larkin must be distraught not knowing what had become of him.

'Who started the fire?' she yelled to the man next to her.

'Some lads, I think. They're caught though,' he said as he heaved more water to the man up the ladder.

Christie wondered who had caught them, but then, as the flames were nearly out she decided to look for Tommy. She took the lantern and carefully walked round the garden calling him. She slipped once or twice as the slopping of the water had made the earth muddy but she managed to save herself from falling full length. She brushed her long hair out of the way as she called and called.

The men by now had doused every bit of the thatch and checked that the smouldering remains would not be rekindled. Fortunately, there was no wind that night. No one could do anymore until daylight, so the men began to make their way home. They said they would return later to help tidy it all. Christie, having called Tommy over and over again as she looked for him with no results, came to the conclusion he had either perished in the fire or had been frightened and run away. Tears came and ran down her cheeks. Poor Tommy! She went back to where Len and his horse and cart were waiting and she was just going to climb up when a dark shape pushed at her legs. Christie looked down. Was it Tommy? She bent and saw the big green eyes looking at her and a great purring coming from his throat. She picked him up and buried her face in his fur. 'Oh, Tommy, Tommy,' she murmured thankfully.

Len helped her up as the cat was heavy but Christie managed to keep hold of him on her lap. 'Len, shall I take him home with me, or should I take him up to Langley Manor where Mrs Larkin is, do you think?'

'Well, Miss, I suppose she'll be worried about him. I can take you to the Manor if you like. It's not far.'

'I could leave him with a servant or a groom in the stables if no one else is about, couldn't I?' So off they went.

As they went slowly up the drive, Christie noticed the dim light of candles shining in the entrance hall. Len helped her down and said he would turn the horse and cart round while she went to the door. She had no time to knock or pull the bell as the door opened and Martin stood there.

'Good God!' he exclaimed and stood rooted to the spot. Then he saw it was Christie with an armful of cat.

'I—I thought Mrs Larkin would be worried about Tommy so—so I brought him,' Christie stuttered lamely, partly from cold, partly from seeing Martin.

Martin let out a deep breath. 'I thought you were a ghost,' he said, taking hold of her and pulling her indoors.

A servant in his shirtsleeves hovered nearby. Martin took Tommy from Christie. 'Here,' he said, giving the cat to the servant, 'take him to the housekeeper who is upstairs with Mrs Larkin. Ask if he wants feeding or anything. You can then retire—there is no need for us to go out now.' He turned back to Christie. He saw before him a girl with a white face spotted with mud and her hair hanging in rat's tails all over the place. Her cloak, pulled undone by a wriggling Tommy, showed more mud on her night attire and shoes.

'You look a mess,' said Martin softly with a smile. 'What have you been up to?'

'We saw the fire and Len Woods took me. So we helped with the water and I looked for Tommy, that's all. Len thought we should bring him here as Mrs Larkin would be worried.'

'Is the fire out?'

'Yes, the men went home and said they would be back in the morning.'

'You've saved me a journey, you know. I was just going up there. Oh, come here, you poor girl, you look frozen.'

He pulled her into his arms and held her tightly. She gratefully felt the warmth of his body; she hadn't realised she was so cold. As she relaxed against him, it was such a wonderful sensation she would have loved to have melted right into him. She could cheerfully have slept, there and then.

'Would you like to come in and stay?' he asked softly.

She was just going to murmur 'Oh, yes please,' when she realised where she was and whom she was with. She began pushing him away. 'No—no, thank you, Len is waiting outside and Zilpah…'

'Is waiting at home. Yes, I know,' he said resignedly with a sigh.

She looked up at him with a dazed expression on her tired face.

'All right,' he said and kissed her swiftly. 'You had better go back. But listen to me, Christie, sleep late tomorrow and have a quiet day. Now go.'

She nodded and hurried out to where Len was waiting. When she arrived home Zilpah was ready for her with hot water for washing, a hot drink and a warm bed. Christie was soon asleep, cuddling a pillow and with a smile on her face.

When she woke up later that morning, watery sunshine was glinting through the window. She stretched and heaved a sigh. She felt much better. She checked the time and found it was eleven o'clock. No wonder she felt rested. Why hadn't Zilpah woken her sooner? Callers would be coming at any time now. She began to panic as she left her warm bed and then stopped, thinking how stupid she was. This was her house and she could do as she wished and the visitors could call another day.

The events of the night came crowding back to her. Who had set light to poor Mrs Larkin's little cottage? How horrid to do something like that to an old lady. But how had she managed to get to Langley Manor? Did she have a broomstick after all? Here Christie smiled to herself. 'I wonder if things like this accounted for people's superstitions?' But if Mrs Larkin had had a broomstick, surely Tommy would have sat on it too? Her mind wandered on and came to the conclusion that Martin must have had something to do with it. She might have guessed. Then she remembered being in his arms. It had been wonderful. She decided she had better not think of it. She had seen herself in the mirror when she had arrived home and she had looked a fright. How could Martin have...? No, no, no, she would not think of him.

A tap sounded, bringing her back to the present and Zilpah poked her head round the door. Seeing Christie, she demanded, 'And what you doing out your bed? You catch cold. I brought your chocolate and water.'

'Dear Zilpah, thank you. I feel wonderful. How are you?'

'I's all right. You get back in your bed, Miss Christie.'

So to please her she did as she was told and drank her chocolate. Later, in the kitchen, Christie asked if anyone had called but there had only been Ann Smythe who had left a message hoping that Christie would join her and her Mama on Sunday morning at church. They would call in case she would like to accompany them. Otherwise, Zilpah said, there had only been Milton. Christie was pleased to have missed him. Then she took Martin's advice and spent the rest of the day quietly, writing letters, keeping her ledger up to date and discussing with Mary what she needed to take to Bath the following week. It was decided that Mary would accompany Christie to help her choose what to wear but Christie was worried that Zilpah was left on her own. But this problem was resolved by inviting Mattie and Peggy to stay overnight for company.

Next day was Sunday and Christie decided she would go to Saint Peter's and was ready and waiting when Ann and her mother called, as arranged. They trod up the path to the church while the bells rang out and Christie nodded and smiled to acquaintances. She sat next to Ann and Mrs Smythe, then watched others walk up the aisle. She noticed Mrs Hayes and her children who were allowed to sit near the front and Mr Franks with his servant. There was a titter when Milton arrived, as he looked very grand in a bright green coat and wearing his wig. Christie vaguely wondered if he slept in it! He began to walk importantly towards the front but was forestalled by a churchwarden who indicated a seat further back. Then the churchwarden walked slowly up the aisle followed by two figures. One was Martin and, leaning heavily on his arm, tapping away with her ebony cane, was Mrs Henshaw. Martin looked neither to the left nor right but concentrated on supporting his aunt. Only when she was settled in the front row did he look up.

The service proceeded with hymns and prayers. Lucius Thripp had a good speaking voice and also a very musical tenor one. Christie glanced briefly at Ann to see her devoutly at her prayers with a worshipful expression on her face, which made Christie wonder whether it was God she had in mind or Lucius. She would not judge her but she hoped she did not get hurt, that was all.

They sang a hymn. One elderly gentleman seemed not to read the words as quickly as he should. Consequently, he sang the last line by himself when everyone else had finished, much to the delight of some children. The amusing thing, thought Christie, was the way he smiled and beamed at everyone as if it was a good joke. She looked at Lucius who was singing away, his eyes heavenward, but she noticed the twitching of his lips. What it was to have a sense of humour, even a vicar, she thought. But then he was only human like everyone else.

The hymn finished and everyone settled back. It was time for the sermon. Lucius stepped into the pulpit. He stood for a moment until all was quiet and when every little movement or whisper had stopped, he began:

'The Gospel of St Matthew, Chapter 25 Verse 40.

'Jesus said to his disciples, "Verily I say unto you, insomuch as ye have done it unto one of the least of these my brethren, ye have done it unto me."

'An appalling event happened in our village during Friday night. IN OUR VILLAGE! Some thought it a good joke to set the thatch alight of a pretty little cottage occupied by an old lady, or more probably they thought the little old lady was a witch. A witch, ladies and gentlemen, a lady who is no bother to anyone and who, where she can, helps with medicinal herbal remedies. This is not witchcraft, this is using God's natural materials to benefit everyone. In fact, to do this, one has to have a brain. Perhaps that is the problem. Someone was jealous that a little old lady was clever enough to know how to use these herbs and flowers for the benefit of all. I have known Mrs Larkin ever since I came here and I've been impressed by her help and kindness. Some say she "has the sight". Many people have had and still have this great gift. People do not understand it, so are frightened of it. I believe Mrs Larkin has it as she has told me so. She doesn't do anything about it but just accepts it. And so should we. We should be grateful to God that someone in our midst has this great gift. Fortunately, Mr Allard believed and when Mrs Larkin sent a message to him that she feared for her safety, he immediately had her taken to Langley Manor and organised men to watch and wait. Unfortunately, because of the darkness, they couldn't stop the fire being started but two men were caught and are now imprisoned awaiting Mr Allard's decision, as a magistrate.

'I visited Mrs Larkin yesterday at the Manor and she asked me to give you this message. "I would like to thank Mr Allard for being so kind to me and believing in my gift and therefore rescuing me before I was burnt to death. Also I'd like to thank all those that put out the fire and helped to clear things afterwards. My thanks go to Miss Farrell who rescued my cat, Tommy, and brought him to me although it was in the middle of the night, as she knew I would be worried about him. Also, a thank you to Len Woods who helped, too. Finally, my thanks to all those who saw the fire and prayed for me. God bless you all.'"

As Lucius left the pulpit there was a deathly hush. After the blessing, the parishioners filed out.

'Oh, Christie, how brave of you to go out in the middle of the night,' whispered Ann softly.

Christie shrugged. 'Len Woods was with me, it wasn't that horrendous,' she said, wishing it had not been mentioned so that everyone knew.

She shook hands with Lucius like everyone else and then she waited with Ann and Mrs Smythe while they chatted to friends.

The gossips stood watching as everyone came out of the church and noted mentally who was talking to each other. Christie hoped she would soon be able to move away before Martin appeared but evidently he was taking his time. Mrs Hayes and her children came out and Christie stepped forward to speak to them. Then Mr Franks came and joined them. Milton stopped and bowed to the ladies. He told Christie plaintively that he had called several times to see her but had been denied entry.

'That was because I wasn't there, I expect,' said Christie. 'I am very busy, too, you know.'

'But I want to see you about something special. Perhaps you will be there tomorrow? And I was rather shocked you were out so late as the Vicar said. It's not right, you know. You should not do such a thing.'

'Good morning, Milton,' cut in Christie quickly. 'I have to go now.' She turned, looking for Ann, before she said something to Milton that she would regret afterwards.

Ann and her mama were now ready to depart but Ann dawdled a little hoping that Lucius would speak to them again. But he was more interested in speaking to Martin and Mrs Henshaw who had now appeared. Poor Ann, her luck was out this day. Christie, however, was pleased to be avoiding Martin and hopefully a further meeting with Milton.

Chapter 21

Christie need not have worried. For one thing, Martin was too busy with his duties to see her, or that is what he told himself. He wondered what had possessed him to invite her to stay that night. All he knew was that he just wanted to love her and protect her. He would have taken advantage of her sad and sorry state though, and for that he could not forgive himself. It was a good thing she had pushed him away. So it was better if he did not see her again until he could control his feelings. Perhaps after she had been to Bath and they had been apart for a short while he would know definitely whether he would want to go further in a relationship with her. Also, it would give Christie time to sort herself out. He felt she had not told him everything and before he committed himself, if that's what he wanted to do, he would like her to confide everything to him. He would really like to know how she came by that scar. Did that mean he would confide everything in his past to Christie? No, that was different and all over, a wild boy's fling. It was part of a man's growing up. With a woman it was different. Would it always be that way, he wondered? He sighed. He had never contemplated marrying before; none of his relationships had meant that much to him. Since he came to Stanton, however, he felt the need to become a family man. His younger brother had been married some time now with two children and another on the way. Martin felt he had a lot of catching up to do.

So Christie did not see Martin, only Toby, who came to ask at what time she would like the carriage brought round the following day. She had mixed feelings about meeting Martin again and obviously he felt the same. Well, she would be away from him for a while, which would be a good thing for both of them, she thought, but somewhat miserably.

Tuesday morning brought Toby and the carriage. Christie was surprised to see another man sitting by him with a blunderbuss in his hand. 'Just precautions,' Toby said airily when Christie asked why.

She said her farewell to Zilpah and gave her a hug. Zilpah told her she would be busy while she was away. It would be a good opportunity to dust and polish through the house and also she would invite Mrs Hayes' children to come and bake cookies. Little Betsy and Mrs Parsloe, the cook, would visit, and of course, Mattie and Peggy would be there. So Miss Christie was not to worry, she would keep busy and have company. Also, Zilpah added, she might go along to Mrs Larkin's cottage when the men had finished repairing the roof, to clean up inside. Then it would be nice for when the old lady returned home. 'So,' Zilpah finished, 'I shall be all right, Miss Christie. If I's in trouble, I send for Toby.'

Christie waved until she could see Zilpah no more, then settled back to enjoy the ride with Mary. Although the weather was not quite so cold they thankfully placed their fingers in their muffs and feet on the hot bricks that had been thoughtfully provided.

The countryside was altering, Christie thought. Did she detect a little colour around the once stark trees, and was there a softening on the hedgerows? She looked forward to the springtime as everyone had told her how pretty all things were then and the village came to life with the Spring Fair. She must stay a little while longer just to see it all, she told herself.

The carriage progressed at a reasonable pace but it was slow over some of the roads where it was rutted and uneven, and Toby drove the horses carefully. It gave Christie time to wonder what Mrs James was like. Martin had never said and Christie hadn't liked to ask. What was the relationship between them? How did he know her? Well, all would be revealed shortly. She would not worry about a thing and she was looking forward to seeing Bath, which she had heard so much about.

It was when Christie was wondering if it would be possible to stop and stretch herself a little that she noticed some very old buildings, and as they went along further houses came into view. They had arrived in Bath.

'How mellow the buildings look! Is the stonework made of a particular kind, do you think, Mary?'

It wasn't many minutes before they drove into Queen Square with nearly new houses gracing each side. In the centre was a small park with seats underneath the trees. It was quiet and very pleasant. The carriage was brought to a standstill outside one of the houses. Toby alighted and went to knock on the door, which was soon opened by a servant. Christie, followed by Mary, climbed up the few steps and was admitted into a large airy hall. A young man came forward and ushered Christie into the morning room. It overlooked the street and she saw her belongings being brought into the house. Then the door opened and a young lady entered. She was about Christie's height but in her late twenties. She had a round cheerful face framed by fair hair and a lace cap on her head. She ran impetuously up to Christie.

'You must be Miss Farrell. Can I call you Christie? I'm Mrs James but do call me Sally or Sal if you prefer. Did you have a good journey? I'm so pleased you are here and we shall have so much fun going round Bath and seeing all the sights. I love to shop; I hope you do too.'

Christie, rather surprised by her hostess's greeting, smiled and managed to say, 'Yes I do. Thank you so much for inviting me, especially as you don't know me.' She didn't get any further.

'Oh, pooh,' said Sally. 'I'm pleased you're here. Martin said you wanted to see Bath so I invited you. But where are my manners? Would you like to see your room first, or would you rather have lunch?'

'Perhaps see my room and take off my bonnet? Then…'

'Of course, how stupid of me. Come along. I will show you to your room, which I hope you will like. I think it quite pretty but…'

'I'm sure it is,' Christie smiled. Chattering all the time about the weather, Christie's room and Bath, the three subjects became intermingled resulting in a confused monologue as Sally led the way up the stairs and along to the bedrooms. Fortunately she did not require a reply. The room was at the back of the house overlooking a small garden and decorated in pretty yellows and green which would make it look quite sunny even on a dull day. Here they found Mary already unpacking Christie's things.

Over lunch they chatted, or Sally did, while it was being served and when the servant had finished Sally waved him away. 'Now,' she said, 'we can't converse properly while servants are in the room, so we'll serve ourselves. Don't stand on ceremony, help yourself when you want to. Now tell me, what do you think of him?'

Christie, thinking it odd that she should be asked such a thing, answered her hostess rather vaguely. 'Well, I didn't see him very clearly, I wasn't taking much notice.'

Sally looked at her with open mouth, then she laughed. 'I didn't mean the servant, I meant Martin!'

'Martin?'

'Yes, what do you think of him? I'm dying to know.'

'Well,' Christie licked her lips, trying to say the right thing but not knowing what was really expected of her. 'Well,' she said again, 'he is kind and helpful.'

Sally pouted. 'Oh, dull stuff,' she said.

'But what do you want to know?'

'I want to know what you *really* think of him? Do you like him? Love him? What?' She spread her hands.

Christie blushed. 'I—I like him, everyone does, I suppose,' she finished, making a performance of helping herself to a little more meat to cover up her embarrassment.

Sally sighed. 'You're not going to tell me. Oh well,' she shrugged and ate something instead of saying any more. Christie, hoping she hadn't offended her, tried to make conversation by asking: 'Do you know Mr Allard well?'

Sally looked at her for a moment. 'Didn't he say?' she asked.

Christie shook her head.

'We are cousins. Martin's Mama and mine were sisters. Oh, how naughty of him. Who did you think I was?' Sally's eyes were sparkling.

'I—I didn't know. A friend perhaps?'

Sally giggled. 'Did you think I was his light o'love? I'm sure you did.'

'To be honest, I didn't know what to think.' She smiled, feeling for some unknown reason a weight lifted from her.

'Now,' said Sally, 'that is just typical of Martin. He has a mischievous streak, you know. He has to have his fun. Not in a nasty way, I mean, he's never nasty; he can be amusing, kind and helpful, but he can be naughty and he can be stern and strict. As a child I used to keep out of his way when he was like that, you know. He wasn't unkind, but I kept my distance. I expect, now he's a magistrate, he can be quite firm.' She shuddered. 'I don't envy him that job. My Alex wouldn't like it either although he's quite strict, but that's because he has to be in his work.'

'Who's Alex and what is it he does?' asked Christie, thankfully turning the conversation away from Martin.

'Of course, you won't know, will you? Alex is my husband. He is a good friend of Martin's; that is how I came to meet him in the first place. And he commands a ship or whatever in His Majesty's Navy. He is on his last voyage now and is coming home. He will have to work in offices in Bristol for a while but that isn't too far away.'

'I'm pleased for you,' said Christie, smiling. 'It cannot be very easy for you when he is away and I expect you worry about him.'

'Well, yes, of course, but I try not to. But I shall be pleased that he will be nearer to home.'

'When does he arrive?'

'Oh, any time,' said Sally airily. 'I can't say exactly, of course.'

'Well,' said Christie, 'if he arrives while I am here, I can easily return to Stanton. You must have such a lot to talk about to each other.'

'Of course, but he will be pleased to meet you, especially as you know Martin and you mustn't think of returning before next week. And the boys won't be home yet, of course.'

'The boys?'

'Oh yes. I have three, you know, but they are with Alex's Mama at the moment. She likes to have them stay now and again. That is why it is so nice to have you here. It would be like Bedlam if they were home, though.' Then she told Christie that Alexander was aged nine, named after his father, Martin was six and named after his godfather and little Stephen was three, named after his grandfather.

By the time lunch was finished Christie felt she knew nearly everything about the James family and rose from the table feeling exhausted. Sally was an unceasing chatterbox and too long in her company could be very trying. Apart from that, though, she was a happy and loving person and Christie liked her.

That evening both ladies visited a friend of Sally's who was holding a musical evening. Sally said all one had to do was to sit and listen and meet the other guests. 'She never has those singers with high voices, thank goodness, just nice restful music, then supper afterwards.'

'Is it far?' asked Christie.

'No, no, only a street or two.'

'Shall we walk?'

'Good gracious, no. We should have our jewels stolen or something unpleasant. We will each take a chair.'

'Take a chair?' Christie frowned. Did they have to take their own chairs to musical evenings? Surely not! But Christie understood later when, waiting in the hall, the servant opened the door and there were two sedan chairs outside. Christie stepped inside one and sat on the narrow seat. The door was closed and the two men, one fore and one aft, lifted the long poles, which were attached to either side the chair. They walked as quickly as they could to the address they had been given. The chair was lowered, the door opened and Christie stepped out, thankful that the journey wasn't very long inside the stuffy 'chair'. She also felt it was a good thing for the men she wasn't twice the weight!

The evening was pleasant enough. Christie met some charming people and listened to the music. It amazed her that Sally was able to stop talking for so long. She was pleased, however, to return to the house and retire to bed.

The following morning, the day being sunny, the ladies decided to venture into the centre of Bath. Christie said, although she was happy to shop, she would like to take a look at the Baths she had heard so much about and also the Abbey. Christie found that Sally, although bubbly and chatty at home, behaved perfectly sedately when outside. She was also knowledgeable about the history of the Abbey, and she was only too happy to share her enthusiasm with Christie.

They didn't stay too long at the Baths, however, as the smell and heat from the greenish water was not very pleasant. Christie saw men and women being lifted from their sedan chairs by attendants who were noticeable as they were dressed in a canvas uniform. They wore tasselled hats on their heads. As they spent their day in the water, their skin had a peculiar orange look, due to the water's rich iron content. The ill people, suffering from a variety of complaints such as gout, ulcers and various types of sores, were able to sit on stone seats or hang on to the iron rings that were attached to the walls. Some people, it seemed, just went for social reasons and Christie even noticed one or two young men jumping in the water for the fun of it, much to others' annoyance. Christie shuddered. She didn't envy the attendants their job at the end of the day when the water had to be cleaned!

They made their way to the Pump Room where drinking water was being dispensed, but Christie refused the offer, having heard about the taste from Mrs Henshaw. Also, the room, which was unbearably hot, was full of fashionably dressed men and women. So both ladies left quickly and went shopping instead.

Among her parcels, Christie bought clothes for the Hayes children and was pleased to enlist Sally's help. Eventually they arrived back home to have a relaxed afternoon and then prepare for a trip to the theatre.

They were joined that evening by an older married couple, Mr and Mrs Hopper, who Sally had invited as she explained to Christie that young ladies should not be seen in the theatre on their own. A gentleman should be present. They were a pleasant couple and Sally and Christie were taken up in their carriage, but as the theatre was just around the corner from the square where the James's house was, the ride was only short. Sally explained to Christie that as the visitors to Bath during the winter months, like the nobility who hired houses in the Royal Crescent for their stay, had now more or less departed for London, the theatre might not have too big an audience and the play itself would only be a very light one. But she thought Christie would like the visit all the same.

As it happened, Christie found the play amusing and she enjoyed the company of Mr and Mrs Hopper and their hospitality in sharing their box. The theatre itself was interesting, with all the richness of red velvet and golden cherubs that glittered in the candlelight. They partook of refreshments that were brought to them in the intervals.

It was a relaxed and happy evening and they all eventually climbed into the carriage to take them home. Sally and Christie hadn't far to go but as the carriage turned the corner it stopped as another was lined up in front of the house blocking any further progress. So the ladies alighted and, after thanking the Hoppers, turned to walk the few steps to the house. It was then that Sally let out an unladylike squeal, picked up her skirts and ran.

CHAPTER 22

▼

Christie followed at a more sedate pace and as she entered the house saw the reason for Sally's rush as she was enveloped in the arms of a tall, fair-haired man. It was obvious that Alex had arrived home safely. If Christie could have walked past and up the stairs she would have done so, but as trunks, boxes and the happy couple blocked the way, Christie could only stand and wait, which she did with bowed head.

Eventually Sally said, 'Oh Alex, I didn't realise you were so near, otherwise I would have stayed home. Ohhh!' She opened her eyes wide. 'I forgot. I have a visitor. There you are,' she called, and running towards Christie, took hold of her arm and led her to Alex. 'This is Christie. She is staying for a while. She is a friend of Martin's.'

Alex bowed then held out his hand. 'I apologise,' he said. 'I didn't realise.'

'Why should you indeed?' smiled Christie 'I am so glad you are home for Sally's sake. I have enjoyed my stay, so I can easily leave tomorrow. You will have such a lot to say to each other, I know.'

'No, no,' said Sally, 'you can't leave tomorrow. Tell her it isn't necessary, Alex. We are to go to Louise's in the evening, you know, and she has a special surprise for Christie. So she must stay, mustn't she?'

'Of course,' Alex said. 'Please stay as long as you like.'

'You are very kind. Perhaps just another day then?' She smiled, wished them goodnight and mounted the stairs. She was pleased Sally was so happy but felt she could not intrude on them at such a time; therefore she would return to Stanton the day after next.

The following morning Christie was the only one down for breakfast, which didn't surprise her, and afterwards she decided to take a walk into Bath with Mary and order some flowers to be delivered to Sally after she had left as a little thank-you present. She also bought some small pieces of jewellery for her family to take with her to Charleston when she returned. She really wished to see them all again, of course, but somehow felt she did not want to leave England just yet. Why? The reason that sprang to mind she pushed firmly away. She managed to concentrate by visiting a few more shops and then taking a walk in the park. They returned in time for lunch.

Although Sally and Alex were pleasant and friendly towards her, Christie felt she was in the way and she was just beginning to excuse herself on the pretence of preparing for the evening when a servant entered and announced: 'Mr Allard, sir, madam.' In walked Martin.

Alex grinned and went to meet him with arms outstretched. 'Martin! This is wonderful. To what do we owe this pleasure?'

But before Martin could answer, Sally had risen from the table and rushed forward, throwing her arms around his neck. 'Martin,' she squeaked. 'How lovely!'

Christie stood watching. The two men were so different with Alex's fair hair, tanned face and laughing blue eyes compared to the quietly self possessed Martin with that beautiful smile. He saw Christie now and came across to her. She bobbed a curtsey.

'Hello,' he said, 'how are you?'

'I'm very well, thank you,' she answered primly, conscious that Sally was watching with a gimlet eye. She continued, 'And I'm having a lovely time.'

Martin gave her a searching glance and then smiled. 'Good. I thought you would with madame over there.'

'Is everything all right at home?' she looked anxiously at him.

'As far as I know and according to Toby,' he answered. 'And to answer your question, Alex, a little bird told me you were arriving home so I came along to see you. But I shall go away again tomorrow.' He grinned. 'It's great to see you again.'

'Christie,' said Sally, 'I have the feeling we are not wanted and they have manly things to discuss, but what they could be I have no idea. I don't suppose really it is of any importance at all. They just like to feel superior.' And with a sweet smile at both men she swept Christie out of the room.

'Have you eaten?' asked Alex as they left. Martin hadn't so some lunch was brought and as he began to eat Alex poured out wine for both of them. He looked speculatively at Martin.

'You must know a very special little bird who told you about my arrival,' he said.

Martin grinned at him. 'I must, mustn't I? Well, I had to say something. The truth of the matter is that I was told that Christie was in some kind of trouble.'

'Really?' Alex was quiet and thought for a moment. 'Sal hasn't said anything to me and Christie didn't seem to me to be unhappy. She said she would return to Stanton tomorrow as I was here but we didn't detect anything else….'

Martin interrupted. 'That wouldn't upset her and she looked happy enough.'

'But why did you think there was a problem? And, more to the point, why do you have to be the one to care about her? Is she particularly special to you?' Alex lifted an eyebrow.

Martin finished chewing his meat, a frown on his face. He dabbed his mouth on the cloth thoughtfully and as he raised his wine glass said seriously, 'I'm thinking of marrying her.' He took a sip and looked at his friend to see his reaction.

'I see.'

'You don't seem surprised.'

'Well, Sal thought there might be something between you.'

'Why? What has been said?'

Alex said thoughtfully, 'I think from what I can make out it's what has not been said that intrigues her. But then women are a bit odd like that, aren't they? Why is Christie in danger? Who said so?'

'I have had a Mrs Larkin, an old lady from the village, living at the Manor until she is able to return to her own cottage again. Two fellows tried to burn it down, and her, because they thought she was a witch. Fortunately, she can foretell the oncoming of trouble sometimes and we were able to move her to the Manor in time. We caught the two men as well. But it was Mrs Larkin who came to me last night before I went to bed and said she could feel that Christie was in trouble. So that is why I came. But I didn't want to say anything until I knew. Sorry if I'm in the way but I can return tomorrow.'

'You know you are always welcome. I believe Sal said we are to go to Louise's tonight and you know her. It should be a pleasant evening, so do accompany us.'

'Of course I remember Louise. Very well, I will. Thank you.'

'By the way, what happened to the men who were caught? Have they come up before you, yet?' asked Alex.

'Oh yes. They're deported to unknown climes. Why?'

Alex shrugged. 'I just wondered what sentence you had given them. It was a bit heavy, wasn't it?'

'Not to my way of thinking. It was nearly murder and for that they would have hung. I think they got off lightly.' As Martin looked rather grim, Alex said no more, just led the way to the dining room.

After a pleasant dinner in friendly company Martin, Christie, Alex and Sally made their way to Louise's house. Martin was his usual relaxed self but he kept his wits about him with regards to Christie. Was anything wrong and would there be danger for her this evening? But could Mrs Larkin be mistaken for once? He watched Christie lazily from under lowered eyelids as they travelled in the carriage. Alex kept an eye on everyone, especially Sally who was chattering away like a colourful magpie. Christie listened half-heartedly to her as she found that although extremely kind she was very wearying. She glanced briefly at Martin who smiled gently back at her. Why had he really come? She didn't believe for one minute that he had heard that Alex was home. Was he worried as to what she was doing and if she was enjoying herself or not? She couldn't think so. Or was he worried that they were going to places they shouldn't? No, that was silly. He probably wasn't that interested in what she did, anyway. Did he care? She didn't know. The thoughts jostled inside her head and by the time Louise's house was reached she felt drained. However, at the sight of a number of people entering the large house all beautifully dressed, her spirits revived somewhat and she looked forward to the evening.

Louise was an older lady renowned for her suppers and entertainment. She welcomed Christie warmly and said she had a lovely surprise for her later on. Christie said the right words and wondered why she had been singled out for such a special treat of some kind. Perhaps it was because she was from the Americas. The rooms looked elegant with chandeliers and rich furnishings in red and gold. These were enhanced by the guests who wore a variety of colours and looked like large butterflies in the myriad of candles and reflections in the mirrors.

Sally and Alex knew most of the guests to whom Christie and Martin were introduced, so there was much bowing and curtseying. Soft music played in another room. At first Christie thought it all delightful but after a while, what with the mixture of perfumes and heat of the room, trying to remember names, the endless curtseying and saying the right things began to make her head whirl. She wondered why, as she was used to gatherings similar to this at home. Perhaps it was because of the lack of space and air, she thought, and then it dawned on her that since she had been living in Stanton, she had become used to the open countryside. No wonder Martin preferred it. She wondered where he was and saw him talking to a group of people. At that moment, as though he knew, he looked up and met her gaze. Then, as he was about to move towards her, Louise was by her side.

'Now, Miss Farrell, the time has come. Everyone is present, so if you wait here I will take them into the other room. Come along everyone,' she called.

They all wondered what was going to happen and words like 'a surprise!' was on everyone's lips.

Martin waited with Christie while the room emptied. Then Louise came back. 'Promise not to look, Miss Farrell, keep your eyes closed and we will lead you into the next room. It is so exciting!'

So Christie was led by Martin on one side and Louise on the other. In the next room an aisle had been made in the centre leading to a figure surrounded by young ladies. Christie's eyes were closed as promised, a smile on her lips. Everyone was hushed. She could feel the tension in the room and the suppressed excitement.

Then Louise said with a flourish: 'Now you can both open your eyes.'

Christie's eyes flew open and her smile immediately disappeared. She recognised the figure and felt the blood drain from her face and she began to shake. Recovering momentarily, she breathed the name faintly of the man standing in front of her: 'Joel.'

There was not a rustle or a murmur in the room. Even Joel seemed stunned. He was the first to recover, however. 'Well, well,' he drawled, 'my affianced bride.'

The young ladies who had been with him gave a disappointed 'Oh'. Others began to clap and some murmured 'Ahhh!,' thinking it was all so romantic.

Christie, having felt faint with shock a moment ago now partially recovered. Her colour changed from white to pink as anger began to creep through her body. She managed, in a shaky but clear voice to say: 'How dare you say that to me? I hoped never to see you again.'

Joel strolled nearer to her. He was just the same as he used to be, slightly intoxicated, with that smile on his lips. If anything, he looked thinner in the face with the lines of depravity that go with loose living, everything that Christie despised.

Joel put out his hand to touch her face, a look of near triumph on his.

'Don't you dare touch me,' she said.

He laughed. 'Ah, I forgot,' drawled Joel nastily, 'you prefer big, black men, don't you?'

There were gasps from Louise's guests as Joel again put out his hand to touch her. This time, however, Martin delivered a stinging blow to Joel's face, with the full force of his arm behind it.

'You heard what the lady said,' Martin spoke quietly but with clarity so that everyone heard.

Immediately, Alex was behind him. 'Martin,' he began.

'I think this er—gentleman deserves a thrashing,' continued Martin. 'Then he might behave himself and watch his words.' He didn't take his eyes from Joel's face.

'Well, well,' began Joel, 'do you propose a duel, I wonder?'

'Where and when you like,' said Martin.

Christie, looking desperately from one to the other, couldn't really understand what was going on. She was shocked at seeing Joel again, at the words he had uttered, and was totally bewildered. And now, what was Martin about? She looked round blindly and Sally, now seeing the trouble in her face, came and began to lead her away into the other room where she was helped gently to a chair and given a glass of wine.

Eventually, the sound of voices and music playing began once more and Louise came bustling in. 'Oh, my dear, I am so sorry.' She said this more to Sally than Christie. 'I met him earlier and he told me he was to marry Miss Farrell and I put two and two together and I…I…' She dabbed at her eyes.

'It's all right, Louise,' said Sally, 'but I have to take Christie back home. Where are Alex and Martin?'

'Arranging a duel and it is all my fault. I feel terrible.'

At last the men said their goodbyes and the carriage was called for. In silence they returned home. Christie was led into the withdrawing room and Sally fussed over her until she was recovered from the shock. Then Christie looked up at Martin. He was pleased to see the dazed expression had left her.

'What happened?' she asked.

'Nothing for you to worry about,' Martin replied shortly.

'Martin, please tell me. I must know. Are you to meet Joel?'

He looked at her speculatively, then said simply, 'Yes.'

'Please don't. I don't want you to.'

'I have to now—it is agreed. Why?'

Christie hung her head. She couldn't say that if he were killed she would die, or let him know how she felt about him now in front of Sally and Alex.

Sally broke in, 'When is this to be, Martin?'

'Tomorrow morning. As I had planned to return to Stanton tomorrow I didn't see why I should alter my arrangements. I shall take you back with me, Christie.'

Christie just nodded. After a few minutes she looked up. 'If I may,' she swallowed hard, 'I would like to explain about—about Joel Winthrop. What he said about me wasn't true but I can't prove it, of course. However, when you have heard the full story you can judge for yourselves. You can also check a lot of things with Zilpah too. She's the black lady who came over with me, you know.' She looked at Sally and Alex.

'I think we can believe you dear,' said Sally.

'Martin?'

'Tell us,' he said briefly.

'Well, we have a large plantation house. Joel lives at the one next to us but it is a long way away, not like houses here,' she began. Then she explained about her family, servants and workers. She went on: 'To make things secure for my sisters' futures, Papa wanted me to marry Joel so that both plantations could join together and be more productive, so I tried to do what Papa asked. Joel was attractive and amusing when I did meet him. As he was older than us girls we had seen hardly anything of him during the time we lived there, so we knew nothing about him really.' She then explained about the outings and how she thought that it could be a happy marriage and he would change.

'But that was rather naïve of me, wasn't it?' She went on to tell them of the invitation to stay with the Winthrops' and how she was surprised at the treatment of Mrs Winthrop. Also how the house had needed attention as no money seemed to have been spent on it for years. She told them that then she had come to the conclusion that Joel and his father were gamblers.

'Joel didn't pay me any particular attention. I had the feeling he didn't even like me. As far as I could discover they just wanted me for the dowry I would bring to the marriage. So the following morning I decided to return home but not before I had seen their workers. Whenever I had asked about them, the subject was changed. So I thought I would go and see for myself, without anyone's knowledge. I bought some fruit, like we did at home, and some cookies, and I went to meet them. I was in for a shock. The cotton fields were neglected and so were the black people. They were undernourished and with a haunted look I shall never forget.'

She dabbed at her eyes and swallowed hard. Sally offered her some wine and stroked her back for comfort. She managed to continue. 'A thin little black boy took me to where they lived. They had no food and no proper shelter in which to live or anything to use for cooking. Then I saw Joel. He had been with one of the young black girls and he was drunk. She slunk away. There were many children who weren't black. I learned later that they had been fathered either by Joel or his father. Of course, Joel was annoyed at seeing me and decided to take his anger out on the child with his whip. I just couldn't stand by and let this happen, it could have killed the boy. So, like anyone else who was human, I shielded him with my body. Joel struck twice. I—I didn't think he would. Not at me. But I was wrong and he did.' Her voice broke and suspended with tears.

It was quiet and no one spoke. Christie continued. 'I must have fainted, from shock, I suppose. I didn't know any more until I awoke in my bed at home. Evidently the black people had cared for me when Joel left and they managed to get word to Joseph. He is the head of our workers and I have always known him. He came and carried me all the way to my home.'

Christie continued and told them how Zilpah had looked after her but she had just wanted to die. Consequently, she didn't leave her room until Zilpah had fetched Grandmama. 'She organises everyone and is a dear. Zilpah thinks she is wonderful and calls her the "Gran'ma lady". It was her idea I came to England to Cousin Amelia. So that is why I'm in England. Papa writes and tells me how he has helped the workers and they are much happier. Also, I believe the Winthrops have left Charleston too.'

By the time she was finished Christie felt near to collapse but she hadn't the energy to excuse herself and go to her room, as she would have liked. So she mopped her face as well as she could, then found herself taken into a pair of firm and loving arms. 'It's all right, sweetheart, everything is all right now,' Martin's voice crooned softly. She rested thankfully against him, feeling his warmth that soothed and relaxed her.

After some minutes she began to recover slightly and more recent thoughts came to mind. She looked up, pushing him away a little. 'But what are you saying? Everything is not all right. You are to meet Joel tomorrow. Please don't, Martin, he might kill you.'

'If I don't kill him first,' said Martin grimly. 'Besides, a gentleman doesn't cry off, you know.'

'But something must be done,' Christie looked round hoping for agreement from Alex but he and Sally had left the room. When, she didn't know, she hadn't heard them leave.

'Don't think about it any more and we'll go back to Stanton later tomorrow,' soothed Martin.

'It's all my fault. I'm sorry, so sorry,' she whispered.

CHAPTER 23

▼

It was little wonder that Christie hardly slept that night. The amount of sleep she did have was haunted by a mixture of faces, Joel's in particular, that grinned and liquefied before her eyes. The noises that accompanied them were so discordant that she awoke with her hands over her ears. She tried, therefore, to keep awake and tossed and turned until the bedclothes were twisted and scattered and damp with perspiration. Consequently she was out of bed as the morning broke. She sat and shivered, looking out of the window and wondering what she could do to help Martin.

Could she go and talk to Joel? Would it do any good? She tried to think but she was too tired. After some time she realised she didn't even know where the duel was to take place. Martin had been careful not to tell her any details.

She heard a door close, albeit softly. She moved quietly and opened her bedroom door and looked out on to the landing. Someone was moving down the stairs. She then heard the outer door open and close, and muted voices. She decided she couldn't do anything to help Martin but sit and wait and pray for his safe return.

Meanwhile, Martin and Alex were on their way to the meeting place. It wasn't too far. They passed the Royal Crescent and went a little further where there was open countryside.

'How are you feeling?' Alex enquired.

'All right,' Martin answered grimly.

'And will you aim to kill?' Alex enquired matter-of-factly.

'What would you do, if he had treated Sal as he has done Christie?'

Alex just nodded and no more was said on the subject.

They were the first to arrive at the appointed spot, a flat open area of grass that was still damp with dew. Dark trunked trees flanked the area. The morning light, white with a tinge of the sun, heralded a fine day. As the morning was chilly they waited for the others to appear before climbing down from the carriage. Martin looked unconcerned but Alex knew his friend well and judged correctly in thinking that he was angry more than anything.

'How long is it since you used a pistol?' he asked him.

Martin shrugged. 'I don't make a habit of it. But more recently than using a sword.' He flashed a smile at Alex. 'But actually I'd really like to use a whip on him.' Alex nodded in agreement.

Another carriage appeared and a tall man with a leather bag alighted. It was the Doctor. He bade them 'Good morning', looked at Martin and then continued to talk about nothing in particular.

It was two minutes after the appointed time when a third carriage arrived. Joel's second jumped out followed more slowly by Joel. He seemed to walk very carefully. The seconds and the Doctor met briefly to examine the duelling pistols that Joel's second had produced to make sure they were exactly the same. Joel was offered the case first and he chose one. Martin took the remaining one. The seconds marked the paces and Joel had the right to fire first.

Martin stood sideways on so that the target was more difficult to aim at. At the given signal Joel stood and aimed his pistol. Martin gritted his teeth and stood still. Joel stood with his arm outstretched, but it wavered. Good God! Was he still drunk? Joel lowered his arm then tried again. 'Tell him to stand still,' he shouted.

'He is standing still!' yelled his second. 'Shoot.'

Joel did. The bullet sped forth, missing Martin by a yard to his left. It embedded itself in a tree trunk. Then it was Martin's turn.

Joel stood waiting, making no effort to minimise the area of his body. Martin pointed his pistol at his adversary's heart. He stood still, his arm outstretched, his eyes keen and took careful aim. Then he deliberately pulled the trigger. There was a loud crack.

At the same time, Joel, either his brain befuddled with alcohol or just frightened, swayed, with the result that the bullet missed its target, lodging only in Joel's upper arm. He collapsed. The seconds rushed forward and so did the Doctor. 'Ah,' said that worthy gentleman. 'Just a flesh wound to his arm. Otherwise he's fainted.'

The seconds looked at one another, then laughed and shook each other by the hand. 'Well done, George,' said Alex. 'You had better get him home, wherever that is.'

'Do you know, I forgot to ask him,' said George, 'but I suppose he'll tell me when the Doctor's finished with him. You'd better see to your man, he's looking like thunder.'

'What the hell is going on?' demanded Martin when Alex returned to him.

'Nothing for you to worry about. Get in the carriage and we'll be off. I want my breakfast.'

Martin, with another glance at where Joel lay, followed him. He said nothing, only eyeing Alex suspiciously. Inside the coach, on their way back to Queen Square, Martin, containing his anger as best he could, barked: 'Well?'

'Well what?' asked Alex, not looking at him and busily arranging his coat as he sat down.

'Did you by any chance fix that apology for a duel? Because if you did I want to know why.' Martin looked mutinous, his hands formed into fists.

Alex and Martin had often fought fisticuffs when they were younger. They had had many bouts as boys but Alex didn't fancy a fight right now. He sympathised with how Martin must be feeling and it might clear the air between them but the ladies would certainly not like it. So all Alex said was: 'I refuse to discuss it until I've eaten. Besides, Christie will be waiting to see you.'

'She'll still be abed.'

'Want to bet?'

Martin would have lost the bet as Christie was sitting on the stairs facing the door with her eyes large and dark with lack of sleep, her face white, her hair anyhow. When she saw Martin she rushed to meet him.

'Are you all right?'

He glanced briefly at her under lowered brows. Then he said irritably: 'Of course I am. You look terrible.' With that remark he stormed after Alex into the morning room, banging the door behind him, leaving Christie rooted to the spot.

Sally, coming downstairs a few minutes later, found her looking forlornly at the door, tears streaming down her face.

'Christie, what is it? What's happened?'

'He—he…'

'Come up to your room, dear, and tell me.' She led Christie back up the stairs to her room, sat her on the bed, then joined her.

'Now tell me.'

'I was waiting. They came in…'

'Alex and Martin?'

Christie nodded. 'And when I asked if he was all right, he just looked at me and said I—I looked terrible. I've been out of my mind all night with worry and th-that is all he c-could say.'

'Poor Christie. But I told you I used to keep out of Martin's way when his temper was roused. It won't be for long, you know. I expect Alex has annoyed him in some way. It will be all right soon, really it will.'

While Sally comforted Christie, the two men faced each other in the morning room. 'Well, are you going to explain things to me? And if so, it had better be good. What happened between you and your friend?'

'What friend?'

'The one who was Joel's second. Come on, own up, you and he decided on something, didn't you?'

Alex quite calmly looked at Martin. 'Well, when George saw me acting for you, he decided it might be helpful if he did the same for Joel as he had no particular friends present. And Joel accepted him. George persuaded Joel that some brandy was a good thing to steady the nerves, that's all.'

'In other words, he made him drunk. How do you think that makes me feel?'

Alex looked at him consideringly. 'How do you think I would feel if Joel shot and killed my best friend and brought more unhappiness to the girl he was thinking of marrying? Other people have feelings, too, Martin.'

'I am aware.' Martin stood staring at a family portrait but not seeing it, for some minutes. Then he turned. 'I'm sorry,' he said simply and held out his hand.

Alex heaved a sigh. 'Good, that's over then.'

'I wonder,' said Martin. 'You see, I wanted to make sure Christie wouldn't be bothered with him ever again.'

'I know, but it's over. Let's forget it. We shall both feel better after some breakfast.'

So arm in arm they went into the breakfast room. Here they found Sally looking young and pretty with her fair hair in loose curls around her shoulders. She was eating buttered toast.

'Good morning, Martin,' she said, looking at him.

He kissed her on the cheek. 'Where's Christie?'

'In her room. She might be down later.'

Martin gazed at her frowning. 'Do I detect something amiss?'

Sally smiled sweetly at him. 'How would I know?' she said sunnily, popping a fragment of toast topped with a large knob of butter into her mouth.

Martin sat at the table while the servant served him and Alex with slices of cold roast beef. He kept looking at Sally, trying to decide if anything was really wrong or if she was teasing him. Alex sent the servant away.

'Well, do you want to tell me what happened this morning? Or do you men think you shouldn't sully my delicate ears?' Sally smiled, waving another piece of toast at them.

'Nothing much to tell, my dear,' said Alex. 'They each fired and Martin pinked his opponent in his arm. That is all.'

'Oh,' Sally wrinkled her nose, 'dull stuff.'

'You're bloodthirsty, Sal,' said Martin.

'Mmm,' she answered, smiling sweetly at him.

'Sal, stop teasing me. What's the matter? Where is Christie?'

Christie was at this moment coming slowly downstairs looking neat and tidy, ready for the journey back to Stanton. She had had sympathy from Sally and after she had left she decided to pull herself together. She would have to face Martin again sometime, so it would be best to do it in the company of Sally and Alex. Also, she should eat something before the journey ahead. So before Sally could answer Martin about Christie's whereabouts, the door opened and Christie herself walked in. The gentlemen rose from their chairs but Christie hurriedly told them to continue with their breakfast. Sally gave her some toast and made a fuss while Martin looked at her with a frown. Christie ignored him.

Breaking the ice, Sally said: 'Isn't this lovely? Martin safe and sound and us all relieved after last night's episode. Louise apologised—she thought she was helping in something romantic, you know.'

Christie gave her a tight little smile and nothing more was said.

Christie and Martin left shortly after in one of Alex's carriages. Christie had thanked them both and said she had enjoyed meeting them. She was sure they would look forward to having the children returned to them and be a family once more.

The journey back to Stanton was accomplished without problems. As Mary travelled with them, not a great deal was said, only general comments made about Bath or the scenery they were passing.

Christie was set down outside her door, which opened and Zilpah stood there beaming. 'Welcome home, Miss Christie, Mis' Allard, sir,' she called and she was soon helping Mary with her luggage.

'No, I won't come in,' Martin said in answer to Christie's question. 'But I will call tomorrow afternoon if that will be convenient?'

'Yes—yes, of course,' murmured Christie. What with the journey and lack of sleep, words didn't seem to register. Martin, looking at her, understood her problem. He felt a little like it himself. All he said now, as he flicked her cheek with a forefinger, was: 'Get some sleep, Christie.' Then he turned, entered the carriage and went back home to the Manor.

Christie talked to Zilpah for a while, telling her about Joel. After finding that everything was fine, Christie decided a sleep was the best thing she could have. After a warm drink and bed prepared by a motherly Zilpah, she drifted off into dreamland.

The next morning she awoke as usual and felt much better. She visited Zilpah and the girls in the kitchen to catch up on the news and learnt that Mrs Larkin was back in her newly thatched and cleaned cottage. Also, there had been callers, the most prominent amongst them being Milton Bush.

'Oh dear,' said Christie, 'I wish he wouldn't. I've a dreadful feeling he wants to propose to me.' This sent the girls into giggles and she had to laugh with them. Then she visited her neighbours and took their little gifts and stayed to play a game of chess with Mr Franks. Mrs Hayes was delighted with her warm shawl and the children with the clothes she had bought them. She went home to have lunch and array herself in the new dress of dark blue silk that she had bought in Bath. Choosing a book to read, she sat and waited for Martin.

It was a little after three o'clock when he arrived. He looked very neat and tidy in a russet velvet coat edged with gold and Christie thought again how attractive he was as he strode into the room.

'Hello, m'dear, how are you?' Then before she could answer, he went on: 'I really should be wearing sackcloth and ashes, shouldn't I? Christie, I'm sorry. I was in a temper and I shouldn't have taken it out on you. I didn't realise what I had said until I was home. I knew something was wrong between us but it wasn't until I sat and thought about it that I realised what I had said. I'm sorry.'

Christie smiled at him. 'It's all right. It was just that I was worried sick for you all night long and I was tired.'

'You look much better now.'

'Yes, thank you. And that's a change.'

'What is?'

'You saying I look much better. You have told me that I looked a mess, then I looked terrible...'

He laughed. 'It was true but you looked delightful all the same. But I am truly sorry. And now you are back to your saucy self again.'

Christie pursed her lips and said nothing, just indicating he should be seated. She had meant the chair opposite her but he sat down on the sofa, taking her hand as he did so.

'Martin, what happened to Joel?'

'Does it matter so much?'

'I think I should be told whether he's alive or dead.'

'He lives. The fellow was drunk. He fainted as I pinked him in the arm. I had hoped to rid you of him for once and for all.'

'I'm pleased you didn't, Martin.'

'Let us forget him. Now, I want you to be serious,' he said.

She looked at him startled, wondering what was coming. He took a letter from his pocket. 'I had this letter waiting for me when I returned yesterday. It is from my brother, John.'

'I didn't know you had a brother.'

'Why should you? He is a few years younger than I am and lives in Augusta.'

'Augusta? In Georgia? Why didn't you say? What does he do out there?'

'I didn't tell you as I didn't think it of interest and he was thinking of moving anyway. We, too, are in the cotton trade. But I have brought part of the letter for you to read. You will see why.' He handed it to Christie, saying he hoped she could read his brother's writing. So for the next ten minutes she silently read the letter while Martin watched her.

The letter began with John saying that he and Liz, his wife, were keeping well, also the children. Then he went on: *'As you know we have wanted to move from here for some time now as it is on the edge of beyond. We feel it would be beneficial for us all to be part of a social scene in a small town and better for the boys' education. So I have gone ahead and sold the plantation for a very good price and have bought one in Charleston. I hope you are in agreement with this. It is a bit rundown but as I have plenty of profit from the one in Augusta it will be no problem to put all to rights. There has been trouble with the black slaves evidently but the owner of the plantation next to me has explained about the Winthrops, who were very cruel people. So I hope to be a kinder employer.*

'You mention in your last letter that a Miss Farrell is a friend of yours? The Farrells own the next plantation to ours and I have found them all very pleasant and helpful. I think your Miss Farrell is the one who was treated badly by the Winthrops.'

There were more personal messages from the children so Christie handed the letter back, her eyes shining. 'Oh, Martin, how wonderful! Your brother will be kind to the workers and the house will be in good condition again. I haven't heard from Papa recently. I expect he's busy but I have heard from Emma who mentioned that the Winthrops had left. I wonder where they've gone and if Joel knows.'

'Are you worried?'

'Not really.'

'Good. But I thought you would like to know that John is in the Winthrops' house and he confirms your story. I believed you, of course, but I wanted to prove to you that you do not have to worry whether I believe you or not now.'

'Thank you, Martin.'

'But that wasn't my whole reason for coming to see you. You see, I love you dearly and I would be very proud to make you my wife. So...,' he slipped on to one knee in front of her, 'will you marry me, Christie?'

She looked into his eyes that were on a level with hers and smiled. 'Oh, Martin, I would love to marry you,' she replied simply, placing her arms around his neck. 'But...'

'But?'

'What about this?' She indicated her scar and looked anxiously at him. 'Would you mind it?'

'Of course not. I hardly notice it. Remember the allegory?'

She nodded.

He was back on the sofa and had her in his arms in one swift movement. When he had finished kissing her, he delved into his pocket and brought out a small box, which he handed to her. She opened it to behold a sapphire ring.

'The colour of your eyes,' he said.

'Oh, oh, Martin, it is beautiful. Thank you.'

A little later, Martin said he had to leave. 'Sorry, m'dear, but I have work to do and letters to write, but I will see you tomorrow.'

Christie nodded. Then she asked demurely: 'And have you no poem to quote me, sir, on this auspicious occasion?'

Martin stood and thought. 'Ah, yes, I know.' There was a decided twinkle in his eyes as he began:

> 'My love in her attire doth show her wit
> It does so well become her.
> For every season she has dressings fit
> For winter, spring and summer.   (He moved towards the door.)
> No beauty she doth miss   (He opened the door and went out.)
> When all her clothes are on
> But beauty's self she is   (His head peered round the door.)
> When all her robes are gone.'

He disappeared quickly, closing the door. The next thing he heard was a decided thump against it. Christie had thrown her book. Martin grinned.

Chapter 24

Christie was immensely happy. She had never felt like this in all her life and she just wanted to laugh and sing. Even her feet seemed to dance along. She forgot how she looked, about Joel and the recent unpleasantness, because she was loved by Martin and was contented to be in his company, as he seemed to be in hers. It was a magical time and even the sun seemed to shine stronger now she was so cheerful. They went riding together or, with Polly in attendance, just walking in the countryside. This was now definitely showing signs of life with the fresh green tips of leaves and buds on the trees and peeping spikes of citron stalks which heralded the coming of spring flowers and plants.

Christie had written home to tell Papa and the girls her news and saying she hoped they would be pleased for her. She wrote a special letter to Grandmama. She was so looking forward to their return letters but knew she had to wait some time for those.

Of course, Zilpah was delighted and went around the house singing in her usual musical fashion. She also hugged Christie a lot and teased her incessantly. 'Poor Milton,' she would say, 'he go into a decline.'

One day when Martin called he suggested they should host a special dinner for a few friends to celebrate their betrothal. Also, he said, he should visit Lucius to ask him to officiate at their wedding.

'When shall we be married, Martin? I must let Mr Wicks know about vacating the house.'

'Oh, he already knows.'

'How? I haven't told him.'

'Um—no—I have. You see, it is my house; in fact, I own these three houses. So there is no problem.'

'Well, I might have known, I suppose, if I'd thought harder. This house was made ready for me rather quickly, wasn't it?'

'Poor Christie. Such a sad little person you were then. I had to do something, didn't I? I didn't turn anyone out, you know. It just so happened that someone had left, so there was no problem. As to our wedding day, if you agree, I thought when Stanton has its Spring Fair. If we can attend and supply food and wine for the whole village, they can all celebrate on the village green. In that way no one will be left out. We can have a quiet ceremony with just close friends.'

'It sounds like a very good idea. Will I enjoy the Spring Fair?' she asked with a smile.

'Of course, everyone does. It is an event that all the villagers look forward to every year. Besides, I want to buy you something special.'

'Oh?' Christie asked suspiciously, seeing Martin's lips twitch.

He looked blandly at her. 'We shall visit the pig pieman,' he said.

'And why would I like a—a pig pie?' she asked, wrinkling up her nose.

Martin laughed and took her hands. 'He doesn't sell pig pies, my love, but the most delicious pig-shaped sweetmeats. In fact, I think we can both have one.'

'I see what it is,' said Christie severely, 'you are holding a pistol to my head. If I cry off from marrying you, I don't get my sugar pig!'

With a whoop of laughter he swept her into his arms and kissed her.

A few evenings later Christie, accompanied by Zilpah, rode in the carriage Martin had sent for them to attend the betrothal dinner at Langley Manor. She wore a silk dress the colour of rubies trimmed with much cream lace and Zilpah wore her best red dress too. The servants were to have their own celebration below stairs. They were both excited and Christie wondered if Toby was the cause of Zilpah's high spirits. There were many people Christie knew. There was Mrs Henshaw, of course, who greeted her with a smile and said how pleased she was at the news. She had her friends round her, including Mrs Larkin, as she had taken a liking to her when she had stayed with them. Christie also met Sally and Alex again who both kissed her on the cheek and said how delighted they were at the news but not surprised. Lucius Thripp was present, and also Ann Smythe, who looked particularly pretty in a primrose and white gown. Christie hoped Lucius was impressed. There were other friends of Martin's, some of whom Christie had met before.

So it was a merry crowd who sat down to dine. The table looked magnificent with silver candelabra and dishes. Christie noticed some familiar food and suspected that Zilpah had been busy with her special recipes. 'She must be friendly with the cook as well as Toby,' thought Christie.

The servants served the food competently and quietly and the wine flowed. From somewhere, soft music played. Christie thought it all wonderful and everyone was smiling and in high spirits. The dinner took an age but at last it finished with a toast by Alex to the betrothed couple. Then Mrs Henshaw led the ladies to the withdrawing room, leaving the men to their brandy and port.

With Sally by her side Christie was pleased to sit and chat quietly with her. Sally said, 'We are so pleased you are to marry Martin, you know. We both think you will deal famously together. I expect you're sad that your family won't be present, though.'

'Yes, I am. My sisters would love to be at the wedding. But, of course, Martin would like his brother present, too. We think that after a short while we will go and visit them all. I really would like that. And Martin says there is no reason why we cannot visit every year and they can visit us. It will be lovely.'

Sally gripped her hand. 'It sounds wonderful. I am pleased for you, love.'

The gentlemen joined the ladies and there was general chatter to the background of music. A little sedate dancing took place and the whole room echoed with laughter and happiness. The temperature rose and the ladies, and some gentlemen, made vigorous use of their fans.

It was in the midst of all the revelry that the double doors at the end of the room were flung open with great force, resulting in them crashing hard onto the wall either side. The music stopped abruptly and the dancing couples gradually came to a halt, wondering what had happened. They soon found out, as with mouths agape, they stared at the dishevelled figure that had appeared. It was Joel with a pistol in each hand.

'Where is he? Where is she?' he yelled and fired once at the ceiling, looking round him meanwhile.

There were screams and sobs from the frightened assembly; some were transfixed as if turned to stone and Christie, whose heart had jumped into her mouth, looked for Martin. Fortunately he was standing nearby. All she thought of was to protect him. She moved slowly and stood in front of him, but he gently moved her to one side with a smile and a murmur of reassurance. At the same time Alex moved forward carefully, not wanting to antagonise the mad figure wielding firearms. The silence seemed to go on for a long time, although it was only a matter of seconds.

Joel saw Alex walking towards him and then noticed Martin's movements. He waved his pistol first at one and then another. Christie wanted to scream but stifled it by placing her fist into her mouth.

Joel seemed to come to some decision and pointed his pistol at Martin. 'I won't miss this time!' he shouted drunkenly, and concentrated his entire mind on aiming his pistol at Martin's chest.

It was at this moment that a diversion occurred. They had all reckoned without Zilpah. That lady, in her bright red dress, now marched through the doorway brandishing a large copper saucepan. Without hesitation she thwacked Joel over the head with it, and he collapsed immediately onto the floor in a heap. Toby appeared then, carrying a white cloth, which looked suspiciously like the one from the dining table. He threw it over Joel, and picked him up in his strong arms as though he were a swaddled baby and carried him from the room.

Zilpah, in the act of closing the doors as she left, looked up and saw everyone standing like statues, staring at her. She flashed a huge smile of her white teeth, bobbed a commendable curtsey and retreated with bottom waggling.

After a minute everyone quickly came to life again. Some began to laugh and others clapped their hands. 'Martin,' called a voice, 'the entertainment was delightful—and how original!'

The music began to play once more and after seeing everyone was happy again, Martin and Alex went to investigate what was happening to Joel. They were surprised to see that Toby was in the act of placing him in a carriage with two footmen standing by. Zilpah, organising the whole procedure, stood with her hands on her hips.

Martin cleared his throat. 'Zilpah, what is happening?'

'Mis'Allard, sir. Dis man is bad. Miss Christie don't want to know him no more. We get rid of him.' She looked at Martin, frowning.

'And what are you proposing to do with him?' asked Martin. He had visions of them tipping Joel into the village pond and drowning him.

Zilpah grinned. Pointing to the footmen and Toby, she said: 'If you please, sir, dey take him to Bristol and he go on first ship dey find. Not home, but a long way away. He can stay dere and Miss Christie won't be troubled no more.'

'Well done, Zilpah,' smiled Martin. 'I couldn't think of anything better myself.'

He was rewarded with Zilpah's best smile. 'You be happy wit' Miss Christie, now,' she said.

'Thank you, Zilpah.' Martin smiled at Alex and they returned to the guests.

Christie was waiting anxiously and breathed a sigh of relief when she heard what had happened.

'You know,' Martin said, 'I shall have to watch what I'm about when we are married. Zilpah is very formidable, isn't she? I shan't dare do anything wrong with her around, shall I?' He grinned at her.

'Should we suggest she marries Toby, do you think? Perhaps that would help?' Christie returned his smile.

'Of course, the very thing,' agreed Martin and kissed her.

END

978-0-595-35107-7
0-595-35107-7

Printed in the United Kingdom
by Lightning Source UK Ltd.
104364UKS00001B/322-351